PRAISE FO
EDITION OF *STAR SAND*

"The beautiful image of star sand in this novel rises up from the depths of history and deeply touches the hearts of readers."

The Tokyo Shimbun

"*Star Sand* is a very fine work of fiction that I recommend to middle and high school students. It brilliantly links the story of the American and Japanese deserters with that of a female university student today."

Minako Saito in the *Asahi Shimbun*

"Roger has found an air pocket that we Japanese never noticed."

Hisashi Inoue, author of *Tokyo Seven Roses*

"This novel is a masterpiece of the highest order with its radiant messages sent from the tragic past of Okinawa and beautiful sta
overcomes borders' who h
Japan and the United Stat

University of T

Mitsuyoshi

"This work is extremely dramatic, and what underlies the drama is a worldview based on multicultural tolerance. At the end, that dramatic stage is brilliantly turned topsy-turvy. This is just the sort of stylistic tour de force that can be achieved in the genre of the novel."

Bungakukai Magazine

STAR SAND

ROGER PULVERS
STAR SAND

Previously published as *Hoshizuna Monogatari* by Kodansha in Japan in 2015. First published in English by AmazonCrossing in 2016.

Published by AmazonCrossing, Seattle

www.apub.com

Amazon, the Amazon logo, and AmazonCrossing are trademarks of Amazon.com, Inc., or its affiliates.

ISBN-13: 9781503936027
ISBN-10: 1503936023

Cover design by David Drummond

Printed in the United States of America

Centuries surround me with fire.

Osip Mandelstam

PART ONE

PART ONE

APRIL 2, 1945

A FINE DAY

It all began in the early evening after I made my way to the northern shore of the island to collect star sand. The sun had set some moments before I arrived, and I stood on the shore, gazing out over the sea. It was as calm as I had ever seen it, a vast plate of dark gray with its clean edge, the horizon, bracing the sky. A cool gust of wind struck my face, and I looked around, combing the fingers of my left hand through my hair. My right hand was cupped around my neck. There wasn't a sound anywhere. It was hard to believe that we had been at war for so many years now . . . how many was it? In the life of a sixteen-year-old, even a single year is an age.

I pulled one of my six small milk bottles out of the string bag over my shoulder. Each bottle was capped with a piece of old cloth, held by a rubber band. I kicked off my straw sandals and, bending over, dropped the bottle onto the sand and rolled the cuffs of my mompe over my knees. Grasping the bottle again, I stepped into the surf.

The temperature of the water felt the same as that of my body. I didn't have the sensation of being in the water at all. I had to look down to make sure that I was really in the sea. Three stars had appeared in the sky by the time I reached the mouth of the grotto that jutted out into the water, a place where star sand lay on the seabed.

I looked back at the island. Little Hatoma Isle, sitting by itself, so far from the battlefields to the south, east, north, and west of it. The eye of this monster storm.

The tide was coming in. I would have to hurry. I reached down to the seabed, my head under water as I scooped star sand into one milk bottle after another. Now the water felt cold, and I shivered, shrugging both shoulders as if that would keep goose pimples off the nape of my neck. When all the bottles were full of star sand and the cloth caps tight over their mouths, I waded back through the grotto and headed toward shore.

When I reached the shore, I was strangely exhausted. But it never bothered me that my clothes were wet. In fact, I enjoyed how they stuck to my skin as they gradually dried in the warm Hatoma air.

I dropped down to sit with my back to the sea, felt the top of each bottle of star sand to reassure myself that the rubber bands were securely fastened, and took a deep breath . . .

It was then that I noticed him, a man standing with his back to me in front of a small rocky cliff face some fifteen meters away. I squinted to see him more clearly and shook my head rapidly to each side, as if that would enhance my vision.

The man was standing in front of what appeared to be the mouth of a cave. Funny that I had never noticed this round opening in the cliff face before. I was always preoccupied with the shore, the sea, the sky, and my star sand.

The man was swaying to the left and then the right, on a greater and greater angle, like a clock's pendulum being moved by a forceful and insistent hand. I was sure that he would fall to one side or the other, but he swung back again and again. Then I saw the gun that he was pointing at his right temple. At least it looked like a gun. It could have been a stick, but from the way his wrist was angled over it, it appeared to be a gun. In the dark-gray light, his figure glowed a blurry white—skin, hair, clothing, even the gun all drained of color. He looked like an all-white scarecrow being tossed from side to side by the wind.

A hand like a streak of light shot out of the black mouth of the cave and snapped away the gun. It happened so quickly that I wasn't sure what I had seen. I glanced at the sky, which was now full of stars. I looked back at the mouth of the cave. The scarecrow was falling forward now, as if being pulled by a chain around his neck.

I instantly rose and ran to the mouth of the cave, kicking up the sand behind me, the little bottles in the string bag over my shoulder clanking together as if they were made of metal. I stopped dead in my tracks about three meters from the mouth of the cave. There were two men in the opening now: the scarecrow who had had the gun at his temple, and a soldier. The soldier had grabbed the gun and flung it over his shoulder into the cave, and now he was gripping the scarecrow's chin and lifting his head. That's when the soldier noticed me. He smiled. Imagine someone smiling at another person, a stranger, at a time like this!

The soldier turned the scarecrow's head around so that I, too, could see his face. He was not Japanese! He had light-brown hair and fair skin. This much stood out against the blackness of the cave's mouth. How could such a man be here, in the southern islands of Okinawa, now?

"Is he alive?" I asked.

"I think he is," said the soldier. "Barely. He was about to shoot himself. Can you help me get him inside? He's American, judging from his American Army shirt."

The soldier took two steps out of the cave. Now I saw that he was emaciated, one scarecrow attached to another. The soldier's uniform was filthy, with a hole at the left knee. Again he smiled at me. This time I could see that he had only a few teeth in the front of his mouth, and these were tobacco brown.

"You take his feet, please," he said, wedging his hands under the American's armpits.

We carried the American into the depths of the cave. It ended in a solid rock wall that must have been an inland extension of the grotto.

"Just a minute," the soldier said, laying the man's head on a patch of sand.

I bent down, lowering his legs. His pants were loose. They started to come off, exposing his behind. I gripped the waist of his pants in my right hand and pulled them up before placing his heels on the sand.

The soldier inserted his hand into a niche in the wall and tugged at the rock face. There was a door there that I had not seen in the dim light. It was made of driftwood planks, like those that come off a sunken ship. The door swung open.

"Has that been here all along?" I asked.

"No. I made it. Now, bring him inside."

We lifted the American again. He seemed so light. We carried him into a cave inside the cave. The space was lit by a single candle and was surprisingly large. The soldier shut the driftwood door behind us.

"I wouldn't have discovered him had I not opened the cave on a whim. I sometimes go out around this time of night, when the tide is coming in, to see if I can catch a baby ray that's strayed too close to shore. I saw him just as I opened the door."

We both looked down at the American lying on his back. His tongue was lolling out of his mouth.

The soldier wiped his hands on his sides and, with his index finger, carefully put the American's tongue back into his mouth.

"He's alive," the soldier said. "He's definitely alive."

APRIL 3, 1945

FINE, FOLLOWED BY HEAVY RAIN, THEN CLEARING

I woke up to find the two men sleeping beside each other, back to back, with a space of about fifty centimeters between them. The cave door was shut tight, yet there was a grayish light filling the room. I could see that the door was attached to the rock wall by two chunky, half-rusted hinges at the top and bottom.

At first I couldn't tell where the light was coming from. The air in the room was actually fresh. Then I noticed a small opening in the domed ceiling of the cave. A soft light was filtering through it. I stood up and walked around a wall that curved like a horseshoe, leading out of the room toward an area in back. The narrow, sandy path forked into two shorter paths. On the right was another room, much smaller than the main one, with a low table in it. The path to the left led to a larger area. Its sharply cragged rock walls were dripping with water. I touched the water with my middle finger and put it in my mouth. The water was not salty.

Halfway up one of the walls was a crevice. The morning light was coming through it, streaming across the room and shining onto the path. I carried a small boulder to the wall and stood on it. I could not see out. The crevice was too narrow, and rocks that formed a part of the grotto wall were in the way. But I could feel the morning breeze against my cheeks and hear the waves striking the shore . . . two breaths for every wave.

"Sometimes a coconut crab squeezes its way through there."

It was the soldier, standing in the arched opening of the room.

"Good morning," he added.

"Good morning."

"Do you live on Hatoma? I've never seen you. But then again, I don't go out much. I've seen almost nobody here."

"I live here now. I was on Ishigaki."

"Oh, so you're from Ishigaki, then?"

He lit a half-smoked cigarette with a large silver lighter, studying its surface with raised eyebrows as he took in his first puff.

"Not really," I said. "I just found myself down here because my aunt lives here—or lived here once, I mean, on Ishigaki. She was killed in an air raid in January. I left after that and sort of, I guess, drifted here. Hatoma seems out of the way of battle."

"I see," he said, holding out the cigarette. "Want a smoke?"

"No, thank you."

"You are obviously a very well-brought-up young woman."

"Well, I don't know."

"It's quite incredible, I mean, to meet someone like you down here, so far away from everything. So, how old are you?"

"I'm only sixteen."

"I see. You look older. Maybe twenty, I thought."

"It's the war. You go to sleep one day as a little girl and wake up the next day as a grown adult."

"Hmm, yeah, well. I'm Iwabuchi."

He took a puff of his cigarette and stifled a cough with closed lips.

"Umeno Hiromi. How do you do?"

We bowed to each other.

"Hiromi. Lovely name. How do you write it?"

"Hiro is *yo*, as in *seiyo*. Mi is *umi*."

"Ah, both mean 'the sea.' Maybe it isn't so strange then, your ending up down here at the bottom of Japan. Oh, excluding all of our glorious colonies to the south, of course."

He chuckled, but his chuckling turned into coughing, and after drawing deeply on his cigarette, he dropped the butt onto the sand and buried it with his big toe.

"Is the American man going to be all right?" I asked.

"He seems very sick. But then, I'm no doctor. I'm a poet, or I was, once. Not that you would ever have heard my name or names. Had a few of them . . . uh, names. Changed names every time I changed styles. Iwabuchi's my real name, though."

"I did a nurse's aide course—well, for two, three weeks only, not really a course. That's what I was doing on Ishigaki. I looked after the wounded, I mean, right from the start. They gave me bandages and anti-septic and I was basically treating wounded soldiers from the start. I could take a look at the American, maybe—not that I, I mean . . ."

"But, you know, if you are found nursing an American, you will be killed."

"I know."

"That's what I have expected myself for some months now," he said, glancing over his shoulder at the American in the main part of the cave. "To be killed. By one side or the other, whichever came first. Doesn't even do to toss a coin. My coin has tails on both its sides."

"If you're killed, I guess it doesn't matter which side does it to you."

He smiled, coughing several times.

"You're a very unusual Japanese girl. Come, let's have a look at him. Trouble is, I don't speak English."

"I do."

"You do? How's that? At sixteen? You *are* unusual, aren't you."

I walked past him, back into the main room of the cave. The American was still lying on his back, staring at the ceiling with wide-open eyes. He was not moving or saying a word. The light itself was as thin as smoke.

I noticed the gun lying only a short distance from him. Iwabuchi-san was standing behind me. I turned toward him, as if to say, "Aren't you going to do something about that gun? He might shoot us." He evidently read my thoughts.

"Why would he want to do that?" he said, shaking his head.

We sat down on either side of the American.

"Can't sit up," the American whispered. "I'm . . . too weak."

We gave him water that Iwabuchi-san had scooped into a cup from a pail. The American managed to sit up and drink it, leaning his head against the rock wall. Iwabuchi-san now handed him another little cup, telling me that it contained gruel flavored with wild wormwood. The American shook his head as if to tell me not to translate, that he didn't care what was in the cup. He sipped the gruel, laboriously biting into the pulpy grains of white rice and saying in a soft voice to Iwabuchi-san, who was holding the bottom of the cup in his palm, "Thank you, thank you."

I watched the two of them and thought how odd it was that archenemies should be thrown together like this in hiding, showing each other the palm of the hand and not the fist, straddling the deep trench between enemy and friend. For a moment I became confused and couldn't remember which side which man was on. Their uniforms were so faded as to be alike, their wan faces like those of fraternal twins.

"Thank you. That's enough for now," said the American, wiping his lower lip with the back of his hand.

"What did he say?" asked Iwabuchi-san.

"He said that he doesn't want any more now."

"Would you like some?"

I paused. Actually, I was quite hungry.

"Yes, thank you. But will there be enough for you to eat?"

"Sure. Look."

He lifted the corner of an old, roughly stitched indigo furoshiki. Under it was an iron pot perched on a few burnt-out logs.

"The pot's still half-full," he said. "I usually make a two-day batch for myself at once. Saves on wood. Besides, when I light the fire, I sometimes have to open the door, and I don't want to do that very often."

"Where do you get white rice from? It's such a luxury in Japan now."

"There's a man on the island who knows about me here. He's the only one who does. He gives me what I need. Rice and things."

"It's dangerous for a man like that to help you, a complete stranger, hide. You're a deserter, aren't you. Deserters are—"

"Oh, we're not strangers. He's, well, my uncle, my father's elder brother. So, he's Iwabuchi, too. Yes, I'm a deserter. Even if I went back of my own free will, I would be executed on the spot. We Japanese are not supposed to have deserters. We don't exist."

"Excuse me," said the American. "Do you people speak English?"

"I do."

"You do? That's amazing."

He smiled, but this caused him to drool, and again he wiped his lower lip with the back of his hand. He closed his eyes and seemed to fall asleep.

I ate the gruel and thanked Iwabuchi-san.

"Where can I wash this?" I asked.

"Oh, in the sea. But I only wash twice a week or so, at night. I don't want to tempt fate."

He lifted up another corner of the furoshiki. Under it was a low stack of metal and ceramic bowls of various sizes and a box of bamboo chopsticks.

All of a sudden I felt the urge to urinate. I walked to the driftwood door and grasped its edge.

"Please don't open that. Not when it's light outside."

"But, uh, I mean, where . . ."

"Oh, that place is back around where you were before. The path forks off to the right just before the back room. It's the 'inner sanctum' of the cave."

"I saw a low table there."

"That's right. Well, behind the table there's a hole. First thing I dug when I set up shop here. There's a stack of banana leaves next to the hole. Sorry, no door there. You can prop up the table if you like. I didn't expect guests when I dug it, let alone a young woman."

I stepped over the American soldier, brushing against his leg. He suddenly stirred and blinked, following me with his eyes without moving his head, like a baby does when its mother crosses the room.

"Where are you going?" he asked.

"To the powder room," I said.

"Is there a powder room here?" he asked, giggling. "Sorry, no offense intended. I think I'm next."

As I rounded the curve, the light coming from the crevice in the wall of the back room became more intense, falling in an angled line onto the sand. I heard the American soldier say, "She speaks terrific English," and Iwabuchi-san reply, *"Warui kedo, wakaran."* ("Sorry, but I don't get what you said.")

When I returned to the main room of the cave, a faint column of light dropped from the small opening in the dome of the ceiling onto the sand below. There was a pail underneath the opening, no doubt to catch rainwater that streamed down. Iwabuchi-san was sitting in the lotus position, facing a part of the cave wall that had been smoothed down and polished. Its glossy surface was surrounded by pointed, jagged black rock, a frame around a blank rectangular picture. The American soldier was standing to one side, swaying slightly.

"Can I go now? To the powder room?" he asked.

"Sure. It's on the other side of the low table, in there, on the right," I said, indicating the direction.

"Thank you. You are both so very kind to me. I don't deserve this."

I was about to ask Iwabuchi-san some questions: How long had he been living in the cave? Why had he deserted? What was he going to do if the army found him? But he seemed to be so calm, as if in a trance, as if he was being transported somewhere.

Before I knew it, the American was standing in the arch between the main room and the path leading to the back room, his outstretched arms touching the inside of the arch and forming a *Y*.

"What's he doing? How long is he going to sit like that? I mean, don't his legs hurt like that?"

I was about to answer him when Iwabuchi-san spoke up, without turning his head away from the wall. Though he apparently knew little or no English, he had guessed what the American soldier had asked.

"Well, let's see. Maybe three months, or maybe thirty years. Until they find me here, on this very spot, my bones in a pile in just such a way that they will say, 'He must have died sitting down.'"

"What did he say?"

"He said that he would sit like that until he dies, however long it takes."

"Doesn't he want to leave here and go back to his life?"

I translated this for Iwabuchi-san, who broke into raucous laughter, followed by one loud cough after another. He cleared his throat twice, regained his composure, and, sitting up as straight as an Okinawan hairpin, stared in perfect silence at his picture in the wall.

"Would you like some more to eat?" I asked the American.

"Oh, no thank you. I mustn't eat up all of your food."

"No, there's plenty. And I can leave here whenever I want and catch fish and bring food."

"You can leave? Don't you live here?"

"I live on Hatoma, in an abandoned old house, by myself."

"You don't live in this cave? What did you say the name of this island is?"

"Hatoma. No, I don't live in this cave. I only noticed it when you came here yesterday. I stayed here last night for the first time. We thought you might die. I felt that it wasn't right to leave you in that state."

"Is that when I came here? Last night?"

"Don't you remember?"

"It's all a bit vague in my mind. I swam here from another island."

"It must have been Iriomote."

"I guess. I dunno. It had a kind of jungle on it, so it was pretty safe, most of the time."

"You're very lucky to be alive."

"Yeah, I guess so. I'm lucky to be able to escape from the war. I guess you are, too. Everyone is the same in war, no matter what side they fight for. So, you really live all by yourself? No parents or anything? How old are you? If I'm prying, you don't have to answer."

"Sixteen."

"Sixteen? Wow! I'm eighteen, or maybe nineteen, I'm not too sure what date it is. You seem a lot older, older than me, I mean."

"It's April 3rd, 1945."

"Is it? Gee, then I'm still eighteen. But only barely."

He stared at me like I was a long-lost relative of his, or a friend he had known when he was a little boy.

"Can I ask your name?"

"Hiromi."

"Romi."

"No. Hee-ro-mi."

"Oh, Hee-ro-mi. Hi, I'm Bob. Nice to know you."

He put out his hand and shook mine as if pulling the string on a lamp up and down.

"What's his name?"

"Iwabuchi."

"Oh, that's so difficult. Golly."

"Ee-wa-BOO-chi."

"Ee-wa-BOO-chi. So he's Ee-wa-BOO-chi-san."

"Yes."

"Well, I know that all of you Japanese people are sans. It's like Mister and Miss, isn't it? I learned that from a Japanese soldier we captured."

Suddenly we heard a low grumbling noise. Iwabuchi-san had fallen asleep in his lotus position and was snoring softly and rhythmically.

"I can't believe that he can sleep sitting up like that. Must take a hell of a lot of practice. Hey, look, mind if I get some shut-eye? I'll just lie down over there by the door, where I was."

I walked through the arch and around the curve to the area in back with the crevice in the wall. I put my nose as close to the crevice as I could get it and inhaled deeply. The air was coming off the sea. It smelled fresh and clean. I felt as if I had never smelled sea air before. The sun was shining straight into my eyes. I closed my eyes, but I could still see the edge of the crevice through my lids. My eyelids felt blissfully warm.

"Is Iwabuchi-san going to kill me?" asked the American soldier, standing against the curved wall by the fork in the path.

I turned around. I could feel warm light against the nape of my neck.

"He saved your life, you know. You were going to shoot yourself."

"Was I? It doesn't surprise me. Why did he save me? Why isn't he afraid of me?"

"I don't know. Would you have saved him if the tables had been turned?"

He looked down and started to build a tiny ridge of sand with the side of his bare foot.

"I did that once. I saved a Japanese soldier by letting him go the night before we were going to bayonet him. He was the one who told me about the name thing, you know, the san thing. I untied him and let him escape. That was in Manila, last year, I guess. That's in the Philippines."

"Then how did you get here? Manila is nowhere near here."

"I'm a good swimmer. Oh, hey, I didn't swim all the way here from Manila, if that's what you mean. I was champion of my junior high in every category of swimming. You should see my butterfly. Guess I gotta get better first now, though, before I do any more real swimming. So, I swam away myself early the next morning, I mean, the morning that the guy was supposed to be bayoneted, 'cause people were gonna blame me for sure for his getting away, seein' as I was assigned to guard him. So I managed to hop a troopship out of Manila, and, it's a long story, but I jumped ship again, kyped a lifeboat off this fellow who was drunk as a skunk, I mean, so drunk he didn't even recognize me as an American, and rowed to shore.

I guess it was to that place you just mentioned, the jungle place."

"Iriomote?"

"Yeah, guess so, I dunno. I hid in the jungle there for a few weeks, or months, maybe. Oh, there was a lot to eat, huge crabs in the mangroves, they got claws like goddamn bolt cutters, I mean, and even a wildcat or two that I caught, scratched me up a bit, though. But then people started showing up, and I was afraid I'd be found out. I was living in a kind of dugout covered by palm fronds near a waterfall. There was plenty of water, so that was good. But, after a while, I got worried that I would be found out, and since I have malaria, I picked it up, you know, like outta Manila or somewhere, I was afraid that I would be too weak to get away. I saw this little island and I never noticed even one boat going out to it, so I figured it was deserted or something. So, one day when I had all my strength up, I decided to swim out to here. I saw a couple of people here, but they didn't see me. I've been living for a few weeks, I guess, off roots and rats and, oh, there was a big dead fish that washed up onto the shore, too, that was okay. Amazing what you can do when you have to."

"But then why did you come to the cave? How did you find it?"

"Well, we were taught in boot camp to do our stuff at night, you know, and every night I went out looking for food and things, and I saw him, I mean, Iwabuchi-san some nights. I mean, I didn't know that was his name, but, of course, I wasn't gonna approach him, not on your life. I could see by the old uniform he was wearing that he was a soldier. This is my old uniform, too, though it's really only a shadow of what it once was. Buttons went first. I made these outta bamboo, pretty good, eh? I watched him from a distance and, I dunno, I kind of wasn't afraid of him. All his movements were slow, kind of. So, I figured he couldn't be afraid of anything, or else he'd be jumpy and wary of everything, and, well, I came to the conclusion that he wasn't gonna, I mean, attack me or anything. And I was getting really weak from my fever and, well, lonely. I hate being by myself. It's the worst thing about deserting. So, I guess I decided to go to his cave and just say hello and see where it would get us from there. If he killed me, then he killed me."

"But what about the gun?"

"I should have gotten rid of the darn thing a long time ago. Darn thing's shot, anyway. But they taught us at boot camp that your gun is your only true friend, and I guess it kind of stuck with me. I mean, I hate the thing, but I can't get rid of it. Know what I mean? You kind of get attached to some things you hate. It's really only a decoration, a, kind of, um, accessory, like a heavy medal or something. War is full of accessories. People love that about it. They love the accessories, really, more than anything. So, I guess I decided to just meet up with him and point the gun at myself, otherwise he would've noticed the gun and thought I was going to shoot him with it, and I didn't want that. That's why I went AWOL in the first place."

"So, you weren't really going to kill yourself, then?"

"I was making like I was gonna, I guess. It doesn't shoot, so it was just for show. I thought if I did that, he wouldn't shoot me. I didn't want him to have to kill me. He wouldn't be able to live with it after. I've seen guys, an' I know. Once they kill someone, they're never the same. They may go back home after it's all over, I dunno, but it's not them really going home. You can go home again, but it's not you that's doin' it."

He nodded up and down several times, then shook his head to either side.

"I'm not sure I understand you."

"Well, no matter. Now, tell me why *you're* still alive, Hiromi-san."

SAME DAY

NIGHTTIME OVERCAST

I left the cave and began to make my way home. There were no stars in the sky, only the faint yellow outline of the moon, barely visible under a thick cover of clouds.

In the cave, I had told Bob the story of my life. I wanted him to understand the war that was constantly churning inside me, a whirlpool of thoughts and fears that I could not get out of my mind.

My Japanese father, who worked for Mitsubishi, was sent by the company to Los Angeles in 1922. He met my mother there, a nisei from Santa Rosa, California. My brother Takaaki and I were born in LA. I went to school there and spoke English with my mother. I used only Japanese with my father. We returned "home" to Japan twice in the 1930s, but Mom preferred what she called "the fresh air" of California. She always rushed Takaaki back there as fast as she could.

Then, in the summer of 1941, Father went back to Japan, to Kyoto where he grew up, taking me with him, "just for a few months, a year at the most." Mom and Takaaki moved in with my grandparents in Tarzana, just outside Los Angeles, where there were not so many Japanese living. My grandparents were both originally from Ishigaki Isle.

After the Japanese attack on Pearl Harbor, we had no way to get back to the United States. Father was sent to Nagasaki in May of 1944 to be the foreman or something at the big Mitsubishi factory there, and I suppose that's where he still is now. Mom and my brother were arrested together with my grandparents and they were sent, with all their nisei and issei friends, to some sort of camp in California or Nevada or Arizona or somewhere like that. I don't know if she's still there now.

I ended up living with my aunt on Ishigaki. They began training me to be a nurse's aide there. Then my aunt was killed and I made my way to Hatoma, where I found an empty house to live in.

Listening to this, Bob had just shaken his head, saying "Amazing, amazing" over and over again. Then: "Mitsubishi. That's the company that makes the Zero, isn't it? Amazing."

When I caught sight of the house I was living in, I noticed that there was candlelight inside. By then I was running. My neighbors, two elderly sisters by the name of Yoshigami, were waiting for me.

"Good evening," I said, slipping out of my straw sandals in the entryway.

"Sorry we came in while you were out," the younger sister said. "But we were worried about you."

"Yes, we were worried about you," said the elder sister, bending her head forward to adjust the long hairpin in her bun.

"I'm so sorry I caused you concern. I'm fine. I just went to collect star sand, and, um, I fell asleep on the beach."

"Well, if that's the case, we're relieved," said the younger sister. "Aren't we."

"Yes, we are."

The two women exchanged glances and nodded to each other.

"I'm sorry that I have never invited you in before," I said. "But this is not really my house. Would you care for some jasmine tea?"

"No thank you," said the younger sister, looking around the living room. "We know this house well, though. We used to come here often when Mrs. Gima lived here."

"Is that the lady's name whose home it is? I've never heard it before."

"Haven't you? Yes, that's right. Gima. She had a husband, three sons, and a daughter. The men, even the husband, an older man, all went to the war. The sons were conscripted, and the husband volunteered. She told us that he had volunteered during the Siberian campaign, too. And that was some years ago, wasn't it."

"Oh yes, it was," affirmed the elder sister.

"After her husband and sons left, Mrs. Gima fell into a deep depression, and anyway some bombs were dropped on the island here and a lot of people fled to Iriomote, and Mrs. Gima felt she couldn't stay here alone, so she took her daughter, who was, I think, a little older than you, to live in Osaka where she has relatives. But the bombing seems to have stopped. We haven't been bombed here for a few weeks now."

There was a long pause. Now both Yoshigami sisters looked around the room, as if checking to see that everything they had seen there before was in its place. The candle flickered, though no wind seemed to be passing through the room.

"Is that the star sand you've collected?" asked the younger sister.

"Yes. I have about four hundred bottles now. It's all there, in rows. Some of it is behind the dresser, too, and by the veranda there in the back room."

"Where did you get all those milk bottles? Four hundred . . . that's a lot of little milk bottles."

"A lot," repeated the elder sister.

"Oh, it was when I was on Ishigaki. I met the schoolteacher there. I think his name was Kurume, or something like that. Anyway, he hadn't thrown out any of the children's milk bottles. He'd held on to all of them over the years. He said that each little bottle represented the life of a child under his care. When the bombs started falling on Ishigaki late last year, he was afraid the school would come under attack, too, and he asked if I would take the bottles into safekeeping, because my aunt lived in a pretty sparsely populated part of the island and the Americans were unlikely to bomb there, because, um, it just has goats and that sort of thing, no home industries or anything. But he thought that Hatoma would be even safer because it's so small, so he helped me and we took all the bottles here by boat. Then for some reason I just started using them to put star sand into. There's lots more empty ones to go. I want to fill them all, seeing as each one belonged to a little boy or girl."

All the sisters did was exchange glances, nod, and, in unison, say, "Oh."

Again there was a pause in the conversation. The candle's wax was almost gone, and the flame was about to go out. I stood, took a new candle from the top drawer of the dresser, and brought it back to the table.

"Oh, no. We'll be going now," said the younger sister, standing up. "Please save your candles for yourself."

"Thank you very much," said the elder sister, also standing.

"I'm sorry for such meager hospitality."

"No, don't say that," said the younger sister. "We understand. Don't we."

"Yes. It's fine," said the elder sister, stepping carefully down into the entryway and staring for a moment at my bamboo spear that was leaning against the wall.

There were no sandals or shoes in the entryway except mine. The sisters had come in bare feet.

"Please come again anytime. I will serve jasmine tea next time."

"No, it's fine. But, just one thing," said the younger sister. "Do you mind if I ask you one more thing?"

"Of course not."

For an instant I was filled with apprehension. Did they suspect that I had visited the cave and stayed overnight in it? Had they seen Iwabuchi-san or Bob on the northern beach or elsewhere on the island?

"What are you going to do with all that star sand?" she asked. "Why do you collect it?"

I looked back into the living room, where hundreds of little milk bottles filled with star sand lined the walls, six rows deep.

"Someday Mrs. Gima, or maybe her husband, sons, and daughter will return home," I explained. "That's when I will leave Hatoma. I'll take my bottles of star sand with me then."

"But what will you do with them then, after you leave here?" asked the younger sister in a strangely insistent tone of voice.

Her sister was already outside the house, looking toward us with an expression of vexed impatience.

"Well, nothing, I guess. I'll just keep them. Or maybe I'll just give them to someone."

"Would anyone want star sand? Do you really think you can sell it? It's nothing, really. It's just little fossils."

"Maybe. But it's beautiful. Each individual one is beautiful, like a little star."

"Oh, well, that's fine, then."

That's all she said before turning her back and joining her sister on the path outside.

I glanced back at my bottles of star sand, stepped down into the entryway, and called out to the two of them.

"Good night!"

But they were already some distance away, and, thanks to the strong wind blowing across the island from the north, I doubt that my words reached them.

APRIL 4, 1945

RAIN, THEN CLOUDY

It was already six and considerably light when I awoke. I went to the back garden to dig up some sweet potatoes. A mist was hanging over the island, and the wind was warm, coming, as it was, from the south. I often felt at times like this that I could smell the pungent odor of the mangrove swamps of Iriomote carried over the water on these winds.

Standing at the top of the high mound in the middle of the vegetable patch behind the house, I could see Iriomote through the gauze suspended between the two islands. A sizeable boat had docked on the northwest point of the island, and some twenty or twenty-five people, soldiers among them, were unloading wooden crates and carrying them into a grove.

I pulled two large sweet potatoes out of the ground and picked some wormwood. I brushed the soil off the sweet potatoes with the side of my hand. If I could catch a fish this morning, Iwabuchi-san could make a nice stew out of it all. I removed the large round stone from the wooden bucket in which I was pickling the Okinawan loofah that I had found growing in the garden. Pickled loofah would go well with fish, wormwood, and sweet potatoes.

I steamed the potatoes, wrapped them in a banana leaf, and then put them and the wormwood in a large furoshiki. With the furoshiki tied on my back and my spear over my shoulder, I set out for the northern beach. We had all been told to sharpen a long rod of bamboo, like a lance, so that we could kill the Americans if they landed. I was using mine to catch fish. The mist had turned into a light drizzle. Overcast sky and light rain, the perfect weather for spearing.

Once I reached the shore, I set my bundle on a boulder, rolled up my mompe, and waded into the water. This morning the sea felt cold against my skin. I walked in, shivering, clenching my teeth and rubbing my arms.

Two or three turtles were making their way to the shore. I stood still until they were well past me. A large ray skidded by, disappearing before I could so much as lift my spear into position. The half moon was visible now between the clouds, and I could see a sapphire-blue parrot fish, a plump one, much bigger than the ones I had seen before, swimming along the shoals by the grotto.

I stepped gingerly onto the sandbank that ran perpendicular to the shore. I readied my spear. Though my hand was steady, the tip was quivering in the air.

The parrot fish shifted direction and started toward me. I wasn't budging. It was only two meters away when I flung my spear . . . and hit it right in the side under its left gill! The parrot fish flapped onto its right side and curled its tail inward, as if trying to strike and dislodge the spear.

The moon had entirely cleared the clouds now, and the water was so shallow where the parrot fish was struggling that I could see a trickle of blood coming out of its wound, weaving its way down toward the seabed. The flapping and writhing finally dislodged the long spear, which thrust up before sinking slowly onto the sandbar. I picked the spear up and hurled it to shore so that I would have two hands free to grip the parrot fish. I reached down into the water and grabbed the fish with both hands. It didn't resist. As I held it close to my chest, wading along the sandbar to shore, it shuddered. But I knew that this was only its muscles twitching. It had been dead by the time I lifted it out of the water.

I entered the mouth of the cave, approached the driftwood door at the back, and struck it twice with a large stone. Some seconds later, the door opened. Iwabuchi-san stuck his head out.

"Good morning. You're early."

"Oh, this is not early for me. I hope I'm not too early."

"Not at all. Please come in. Please. Please."

Iwabuchi-san put out the palm of his hand in a polite gesture and ushered me inside. Bob, who was beside the door, pushed it shut. A small kerosene lamp lit the room. The smell of burning kerosene was acrid.

"I can see by your frown that you're bothered by the kerosene. We'll only have it on for a short time. Most of the fumes go out there," Iwabuchi-san said, pointing to the hole in the domed ceiling.

"Ohio gozai-mouse," said Bob. "How's my Japanese? That means good morning."

"Perfect Japanese, Bob-san. Better than mine."

"Oh, thank you. But I think you're pulling my leg."

He was scraping at the wall beside the door with a stone and a wire brush and polishing little sections of it with a thick rag of oily canvas.

"This should do the trick," said Bob. "But we've still got miles to go. Oh well, Rome wasn't built in a day. Keep up the good work, Bob-san. Look, I'm now even calling myself 'san.'"

"What's he doing?" I asked.

"Polishing his wall. Since he figures that he might be here for a while, he wants to have his own piece of wall. Makes a lot of sense. Well, it was really me who started it all off. Bob's clever though. He picked up on it right away. No need for language. We are both *kawazu* (frogs). Ha ha."

"Kawazu? Why?"

Bob laughed heartily when he heard this word, inhaling as he laughed, which made him sound somewhat like a chimpanzee.

"Croak, croak," he said between laughs, busily rubbing his piece of canvas in circles over a small section of the wall.

"We figured it out last night. No need for language with us. You see, Bob is a deserter from the American Army, and I'm a deserter from the Japanese Army. We are both kawazu."

At this, both men burst, in unison, into a series of loud guffaws. They sounded like coyotes I once heard outside Needles, California. Bob slapped his side and dropped the piece of canvas. Bending down to retrieve it, he hit his head against the wall.

"Ouch!" he said.

"See? We are getting our just deserts already, we kawazu!" said Iwabuchi-san. "The wall is taking its justice out on us."

When he heard the word "kawazu," Bob, half-bent over, broke into another series of guffaws, each one louder than the one before. I thought he was going to choke.

"I'm sorry, but I really don't follow this," I said, looking first at Iwabuchi-san, then at Bob.

"Well, as I said, we are both deserters," said Iwabuchi-san. "Apparently, I don't know, the word for 'deserter' in English is kawazu or something like that."

Bob, now standing again and rubbing the back of his head, turned fully toward me and attempted to explain the source of all this amusement. His explanation was interrupted by more laughter, which in turn prompted Iwabuchi-san to giggle, when he wasn't coughing.

"You see . . . wait a minute, this is so funny . . . you see, Iwabuchi-san here and I really can't have much of a man-to-man. All he can say in English is 'sankyuu,' and the only Japanese I know besides 'ohio gozai-mouse' is 'a-ree-ga-do,' which is the same as sankyuu. So I pointed to myself last night and said, 'Coward . . . coward.' And, hold it, I, golly, I can't stop laughing, okay, so he points to himself and says something in Japanese, then 'Coward . . . coward,' only he pronounces it in Japanese, like, 'ka-wa-zoo.'"

At that both men began cackling so hard that they had to sit down. I waited until they both stopped pounding the sand with their fists and calmed down.

"But kawazu is the Japanese word for 'frog,'" I said.

"Is it?" said Bob, now laughing so hard he could barely catch his breath. "But," he continued, wiping his nose on his sleeve and blinking his eyes over and over, "there's a difference. When I point to myself, I point to my chest. But Iwabuchi-san here, he points to . . ." He had to stop. This time his laughter was silent, like gagging. He stared at me with his eyes bulging and his mouth agape, breathing in and out in gasps and holding his palms flat against his chest. "And Iwabuchi-san, he, okay, so, he points to his nose, like this."

Their laughter subsided, and their breathing gradually returned to normal. They were staring up at me with eyes not unlike those of the parrot fish lying flat on the sand between them.

"Well," I said in English, "it's nice to see that the war has ended, at least in this cave," adding, in Japanese, "I've brought breakfast for the two of you. The sweet potatoes, wormwood, and pickled loofah are in the furoshiki. Oh, and I've also got this, if he can calm down enough to put it on."

I took a thin blue-and-white linen sash belt from my pocket and handed it to Bob.

"This is for you," I said.

"Oh, thank you. What is it? Sorry for the outburst. But it was just all too funny for words."

"It's a belt to keep your pants up."

"Now that's something I do need!" He chuckled, grasping the waist of his pants.

"You see the dyed pattern on it? Look here. There are five little white rectangles here and four next to them. See? It's repeated. Five four, five four."

"What does it mean? Why five and four?"

"It's an old Okinawan pattern. Five is *itsu* and four is *yo*. So it stands for *itsu no yo made*, which means, 'For ever and ever.'"

"Gosh, that's so romantic," said Bob, stroking the pattern with his fingertip.

"Oh, thank you, Hiromi-san," said Iwabuchi-san. "You are so kind. Bob is feeling a lot better now, and I think he will be able to eat something. He is frightfully thin. I am so grateful to you, Hiromi-san. You shine a radiant light into this dark cave."

Iwabuchi-san, sitting cross-legged on the ground, bowed his head with his palms clasped together at his chest. Bob, wincing, pulled himself up by clinging to the wall, and once again began to polish a section beside the door, breathing on the wall as if to make it shine like a mirror. Iwabuchi-san rose and untied the furoshiki, sticking his nose against the banana leaf and inhaling deeply.

"Aaah" was all he said, smiling at Bob. "Just like Mother used to make."

But Bob had his back to us, feverishly polishing the one little circular spot of his wall that was already smooth.

"I'll turn off the lamp now. Then the smell of the fish and sweet potatoes will fill our cave. There's enough light coming in now from the dome anyway."

As Iwabuchi-san began preparing breakfast for himself and Bob, I walked around the horseshoe curve into the back room. I could hear the waves striking the shore rhythmically, one for every two breaths as before. I peered into the crevice, which fanned open at its higher reaches. I would have to stand on something to see out of it.

I went to the place Iwabuchi-san called the "inner sanctum." Lifting the low table and holding it with its legs out, I returned to the back room, where I placed the table below the creviced wall. I stood on the table. By putting my forehead flush against the crevice and slightly to the side, I could see a vertical stripe of sea and sky.

The rain had lifted, but a pastel, grayish rainbow still cut across the stripe. From the crevice, all I saw was a rectangle of fading colors against a monotone sheet of cloud. I inhaled the salty air, shutting my eyes tightly and imagining myself somewhere and sometime else, on a beach with groups of people scattered along it . . . men and women dead to the world on their stomachs and backs under the sun, old people staring vacantly out over a calm surf, children building castles with walls and moats in the sand. When I opened my eyes, the rainbow was gone and the vertical stripe of sea and sky was uniform gray.

I returned to the main room. Iwabuchi-san was squatting over his iron pot, which was bubbling with chunks of sweet potato in it. He had scaled the parrot fish and was cutting it into thick strips. Bob was lost in his wall, breathing onto it, scraping at it, polishing it, and pulling his head back to view it from farther away.

"Wonder if this will be to his taste," said Iwabuchi-san, holding the head of the parrot fish over the pot. He was watching the liquid, waiting for a suitable opening to drop in the fish head.

"What do you mean?" I asked.

"This is fish stew. Americans don't eat fish. That's what our officers told us. They only eat meat. Maybe Bob won't like this."

"I doubt that. I'm sure he will be happy to eat it. He said that he eats fish. He ate it before."

"Ask him, anyway. It's only polite."

"What?"

"Ask him if it's all right to serve him this."

"Bob?"

"Yeah?" he said without turning around. He drooled a gob of spit onto his piece of canvas and rubbed it into the wall.

"Go on, ask him."

"Bob?"

"Yeah, what is it? I hear ya."

"Iwabuchi-san is worried that you won't like fish stew."

Bob swiveled around, stuffing the piece of canvas into his shirt pocket.

"I haven't been this hungry in months. Malaria swipes your appetite. Smells great."

"You eat fish?"

"Fish? Sure. Mom made the best gefilte fish in Bensonhurst."

"Sorry, but I don't know what that is."

"Bensonhurst? That's where I hail from, in Brooklyn, you know, New York."

"No, that too, but the other thing, the fish."

"Gefilte fish? Well, it's a sort of, well, kind of, um, you know, you take a lot of fish and you, um, kind of, you, well, you make it up until you get gefilte fish."

"What does he say?" asked Iwabuchi-san. "It seems like he's explaining why he doesn't like it."

"No, he says he likes fish. It's fine."

I watched the two of them devour the stew, popping slices of pickled loofah into their mouths. Not a word passed between them, only grunts of affirmation. I let out an inadvertent chuckle myself, picturing them for an instant as frogs sitting on two lotus leaves in a pond. Steam from the pot rose straight up and out the opening in the domed ceiling.

"What's so funny, Hiromi-san?" asked Iwabuchi-san, pulling a long, curved bone from between his lips. "Tell Bob to watch out for bones."

"Bob, Iwabuchi-san says, 'Be careful of bones.'"

"Yeah, thanks, but I could tell that's what he said. We're doin' fine. I'm doin' just fine."

Iwabuchi-san was holding up the bone that had just come out of his mouth, waving it and saying "No, no, no" in English.

"A-ree-ga-do, Iwabuchi-san. I got it. Bones."

After they both finished breakfast, Iwabuchi-san went to the toilet in the inner sanctum.

"Where's the table?" he said, standing by the fork in the path.

"Oh, sorry. I left it in the—"

"That's fine," he said. "I'll put it back."

Bob was lying on his side, resting his head in his palm.

"Bob, how are you feeling?"

"Never felt better in my life."

Iwabuchi-san returned after some moments, with two pairs of pants, two shirts, and two loincloths draped over his arms.

"Where did those come from?" I asked.

"Oh, from the box by the arch in the back room. Please tell Bob to put these on. He can change in the back room."

"I can wash your old clothes, if you like."

"That's very kind of you, Hiromi-san. I don't know what we have done to deserve all this kindness."

I put their old clothes in the pail, picked up the breakfast dishes and chopsticks, and carried everything out of the cave. Iwabuchi-san shut the door behind me.

Bob's uniform was caked with mud and stiff in patches, and Iwabuchi-san's uniform was yellowed with sweat. I set the pail, dishes, and chopsticks down on the shoreline. But before I could begin to wash, a voice came from behind me.

"What are you doing out here?"

It was the younger Yoshigami sister. She had come over the rocky point and was standing near the entrance to the cave, peering around.

"Oh, I'm doing uh, some washing, that's all."

I crumpled the clothes up so that she could not guess their nature.

"Really? Why here? There's closer places to your house to do it."

"Oh, well, I like it here. This is where I collect star sand. I'm going to do that, too."

"Really? Where are your milk bottles?"

"Over there," I said, waving vaguely toward the grotto.

She squinted her eyes and stared in the direction of the grotto. Then, seemingly losing interest, she sat down on a boulder, took a pack of Kinshi cigarettes and a box of matches from the sleeve of her kimono, pulled out a cigarette, lit it, and started to smoke. With my back to her, I washed the clothes, scrubbing them on a flat rock that protruded from the surf. I crumpled the wet clothes into a large ball and stuffed it all into the pail. Then I rinsed the two dishes and chopsticks, shook off the water, and placed the dishes facedown in the pail. I rose and turned around. My neighbor was still sitting on the boulder, lighting another cigarette.

"You haven't seen any turtles, have you?"

"Pardon? Turtles? No. Not, I mean, recently."

"Well," she said, sighing and standing laboriously, "I'll be getting on home now. Good luck with your star sand."

"Thank you very much. Give my regards to your sister, please."

She smiled with unparted lips, nodded with a short jerk of her head, adjusted the long hairpin sticking out of her bun, turned, and began climbing over the rocks toward home. I waited a considerable time until I was sure she had gone, returned to the cave, knocked twice on the door with a stone, and handed the pail to Bob.

"Where's Iwabuchi-san?" I asked.

"He's sitting in front of his wall. Shh. I don't think it's really good to talk a lot while he's doing that."

"Sure. Well, I'll leave you two alone today. I'll come back tomorrow, when I'll be collecting star sand."

"We're fine. Don't you worry a bit about us. We're like two frogs in a pond."

Bob patted me on the shoulder and smiled generously. He was still smiling his innocent boyish smile, with only his head protruding from the driftwood door, when I turned around at the mouth of the cave to wave good-bye.

APRIL 5, 1945

FINE

This war is ripping me in two.

The Gimas had left a radio in the back room of the house, wedged in between two crates of farm tools. The tools were piled on top of each other and clogged with mud, as if they had been stuffed into the crates in a hurry.

I rarely turned the radio on. Had I expected an announcement one day saying that the war had ended, I would have been glued to the radio day and night. I really didn't think much at this stage about whose victory it was going to be, just about when it all might end. I felt in my bones that this war was going to last a lifetime . . . my lifetime. Then, it would cast a blood shadow onto the heads of all people, including those not yet born. Whether the unborn could ever erase the stain of that blood and rid themselves of its mark on them, or how they might go about accomplishing that, would be their problem, not mine. The stain on me, already reddish brown, as if it had been there for an age, was indelible.

I sat down in front of the radio and turned it on. It picked up only one station. Everything else was waves of static. An announcer was reporting that a major battle had begun in Okinawa and that the imperial forces were repelling the American invasion bravely and successfully.

"The cruelty of the American soldiers is . . . (static obscured the next few words) . . . brutally raping Okinawan women and girls and torturing . . . (again static) . . . they bayonet babies in the air and . . . in the neck and groin . . ."

I leaned forward and turned the radio off. The handle of a bamboo rake was sticking out of the crate to the right of the radio. I grabbed the rake and pulled it out of the crate. Its teeth were entangled in dry, stringy roots.

This war ripped my family in two.

My father and I "returned" to Japan. Where he was, God only knew. I knew that he went to work at the Mitsubishi plant in Nagasaki, but that had been three years ago. Had he been sent elsewhere? China? Korea? The Philippines? Indochina? Was he alive? He would have been proud to die for his country. He had said as much to us before we left America. He didn't want to live the rest of his life surrounded by the enemy, and he made sure that, at the very least, I would not be obliged to do the same.

As for my elder brother, he was nineteen then and could not be ordered around. Takaaki decided that he would stay in America. Father slapped him, once, with some force, on the cheek. This was not a slap to admonish him for disobeying. It was a gesture of disgust, disgust at Takaaki's decision to throw his lot in with "the enemy." Father kept saying, "There is going to be a war between Japan and America. They are forcing us into it. We will give them what they want. You cannot be on both sides of a war." But Takaaki stood his ground. He didn't say a word. He just stared at Father with a look of hatred that I had never seen on his face before. He was a kind and gentle boy, yet the slap brought something out in him that he must have been harboring deep inside himself all along. Father stormed out of the room. Ten days later, Father and I boarded a ship at San Pedro wharf and sailed, via Hawaii, to Japan.

That single gesture, that slap, changed our family forever. Mother could do nothing but stand to one side and sob. She wept for two hours and then went to bed and didn't come out for a day and a half. There was no way that she would ever abandon the country she was born in. Besides, my grandparents had decided not to return to Ishigaki. Mother would have to be responsible for them as well. She didn't even see us off at the pier.

Not long after Pearl Harbor, Mother, Takaaki, and my grandparents were ordered to leave their home in Los Angeles. They were sent to a camp somewhere in the desert. I heard this from my aunt on Ishigaki when I arrived there. Sometime in 1942, she received a letter that had been forwarded to Japan by the Red Cross. The letter contained a single photograph showing Mother, Grandma, and Grandpa standing in front of an unpainted wooden building. Takaaki wasn't there. In the letter, Mother wrote that Takaaki had been let out of the camp "to join up." I was surprised that the Japanese government would allow such information to be passed on. I guess they didn't know the meaning of "join up."

Was it possible, then, that Takaaki was in Okinawa now, killing Okinawan civilians and Japanese soldiers? Or perhaps he would be killed himself. Images of him flashed through my mind like in a silent film: Takaaki stepping onto the beach . . . Takaaki being hit in the middle of the chest by a bullet . . . Takaaki falling backward, clutching his rifle in his right hand, a spurt of blood suddenly appearing in the middle of his chest, flowing down his shirt . . . Takaaki on his back, other soldiers hopping over him or stepping around him, without so much as a downward glance . . .

I knelt in front of the radio and turned it on again, but this time, I heard only static. What was I going to do today? I could remain here in this house, eating vegetables from the garden, sleeping, waiting. I could choose not to return to the cave. Iwabuchi-san and Bob would not have come looking for me. They would have assumed that I naturally decided to save my own skin, coming to the conclusion that helping a deserter from the Japanese Army and a runaway American could lead nowhere but straight to tragedy for me. It would be so easy to stay put, to sit still and let the war's clock tick out. How old would I be when this war ended? What would I have to do to patch the two parts of my family together again, sew together and remake this little, thin, colorless quilt that I called my life?

But, since a couple of days ago, I had two men to look after. Funny. Two men, two soldiers, being cared for by a sixteen-year-old girl. Once I knew of their existence, my choices were taken from me. I could no more pretend that they were not living on this island than I could wish this war out of existence. Under the barrage of static were the same descriptions of horror, the same unspeakable waves of terror making their way slowly forward, a tide that would never ebb. I now had duties to attend to. I had my star sand to collect, for one thing. I needed to have a thousand bottles of it gathered by the time this war ended. That was my goal, come what may. It was my way of defining time, not by giving it a meaning but by marking it. There was no limit to the star sand that could be found in the sea surrounding Hatoma Isle. I could go on doing this forever without having to ask myself where it was leading me.

I fell asleep for some hours. When I awoke, I realized that I had been drooling on the floor. I quickly wiped the pool of saliva up with my sleeve. It was already afternoon, and the sun was beating down on the roof with such force that I could hear the tiles creaking.

I went out to the garden, pulled four sweet potatoes out of the ground, and picked several fat cucumbers. The rains and sun were so strong on Hatoma that you could almost watch the vegetables swell as they rose out of the ground. I wrapped the sweet potatoes and cucumbers in some old newspaper that the Gimas had left in a pile in a small shed by the outhouse, and I placed this next to ten empty milk bottles in my furoshiki. Then I tied the furoshiki to my back, slid into my straw sandals, and set out, with my spear over my shoulder, for the beach on the northern edge of the island.

I walked toward the dock, passing several gutted houses that had been hit by bombs, the names of their owners still on display on wooden nameplates by their front gates. I turned up the main path leading northward. Grasses taller than me lined the path, colored by red hibiscus and the soft yellow blossoms of loofah plants.

There were clearings along the path, with houses set back in them. The biggest house on the island belonged to Iwabuchi-san's uncle. I had greeted him only two or three times, but he always smiled and said polite things to me. I stopped for a moment and took a few steps on the path that led to his house. The house had a shoulder-high wall of piled stones around it and a red-tiled roof. Right in front of it was a garcinia tree that must have been fifteen meters high, with a mass of dark-green leaves clustered around every branch. These trees were the perfect protection against the typhoons that struck the island every year.

I turned back onto the main path, walking into the densely wooded middle of the island and climbing to its tallest point. I could see Iriomote in the distance. The boat was still where it had docked the day before, but now the entire area was deserted. Then, one person appeared on the deck of the boat. I couldn't make out if he was a soldier or not. Suddenly, for some reason, he began to wave his arms high in the air. Could he see me? That should have been impossible, given the camouflage of the trees. He continued to wave like that, in the way Okinawan dancers do, first with one hand and then with the other. I turned away and, climbing down the sandy slope, headed north. By the time I reached the beach, it must have been close to three o'clock.

The light-magenta sea bells by the rocky point were drooping from the heat.

On the beach, I put down my furoshiki and unwrapped it, taking out the ten empty milk bottles. The tide had brought in an unusually large amount of seaweed, which sat in pyramid piles along the shore. I rolled up the cuffs of my mompe, put the bottles in my string bag, and stepped into the water.

The water felt warm against my skin, and my bare feet sank deep into the sand as I made my way to the end point of the grotto. I looked back at my furoshiki on the shore, with the sweet potatoes and cucumbers wrapped in newspaper on it, and waded around the edge of the grotto to the place where the seabed itself was made of star sand. Holding two milk bottles, one in each hand, I dunked my head under water, bent forward, and scooped star sand into them. It flowed into the bottles as if it, too, were a liquid. It took only one scoop to fill each bottle. I pulled my head out of the water and shook it. My black hair, which I had tied up and secured with a long hairpin, came loose, shaking countless drops of water into the air on all sides of me. I could see the drops fall into the water like rain, and I put my head under water again, pulled it out, and shook it back and forth even more vigorously than before, sending a radiant shower in all directions.

I filled all ten bottles with star sand, shaking my head each time I came up. I fastened the top of each bottle with a piece of cloth and a rubber band. Then I retrieved the long hairpin from the seabed and dropped it into the string bag beside the bottles of star sand. When I cleared the point of the grotto and turned back toward shore, I noticed that there was nothing on top of my furoshiki. The packet of vegetables had disappeared. I plodded quickly through the water, lifting my knees as my feet sank deep into the sand. When I reached shallow water, I ran.

Finally I stood at the mouth of the cave. I had suspected that my neighbors, the elderly Yoshigami sisters, were coming to this spot, for what reason I could not imagine. I was the only one who collected star sand on this island. Or perhaps Iwabuchi-san had left the cave and, discovering the vegetables, took them back inside. After all, sweet potatoes would take a long time to cook on his meager fire. I was overcome with fear, and I felt for the first time since discovering the cave that I might lose my life because of it.

I entered the cave, looking around to make sure that I was alone, picked up a stone, and knocked twice on the driftwood door at the back wall. It didn't open. I knocked again. Again it didn't open. I was about to knock a third time when the heavy door slowly opened.

"Hi," said Bob, grinning like a little boy.

"Good afternoon," I said.

"I suppose you're looking for your vegetables."

"Well, um, actually . . ."

"Iwabuchi-san's got them. I told him it was too dangerous to go out, but he won't listen to me, you know. For a coward, the guy's got a lot of guts."

Again Bob grinned.

"No, that's fine. As long as you have them. I'm going to see if I can spear some fish for dinner tonight."

"Okay. Just go, 'Knock-knock, who's there!'"

Bob chuckled, shrugged a shoulder, and shut the door. I picked up my spear at the mouth of the cave and went back to the shore, where I had left my string bag of bottles full of star sand between two piles of seaweed. The entire sweep of the sky was bright blue, with only a single oval white cloud over the horizon. My cuffs were still rolled up, and my mompe and shirt were soaking wet. I waded through the water and entered the grotto, where there was ample shade from the blinding light of the sun. There seemed to be no fish in the water at all. I could see all the way down to the bed. I curled my toes into the sand and waited. I must have stood there for ten minutes before catching sight of a small school of anemonefish. A few were reddish in color, but most were orange with two white stripes circling their bodies. They were all much too small to spear or eat. They swam gracefully around my legs. I may as well have been made of stone.

Again I stood without moving for about ten minutes. I was becoming very tired and was about to turn back when an enormous fish that looked like a sea bream swam into the grotto. I had never seen a sea bream of such size. It looked as big as a valise. It stopped for a moment by an inner wall of the grotto, its jaw gaping and closing. It was no doubt feeding on something in the water that I could not see. Then it turned toward me and started in my direction. I lifted my spear into the air. The fish was now only about two meters away, still approaching. I pointed the spear at it and tightened my grip. All of a sudden, as if sensing danger, it flipped to the side and raced away. I took one step forward and thrust the spear into the water. I hit the fish just behind the right gill! Blood oozed into the water. The fish fell to the seabed, its body shaking in violent convulsions. The sea bream was skewered by my spear, its tip sticking out its other side behind the left gill. Its mouth was agape, and it had ceased trembling.

I went back to the shore with the sea bream still attached to the spear, moved the string bag with the bottles of star sand up the beach so that the tide would not take it, and entered the cave. I knocked twice on the door at the back. Opening the door, Iwabuchi-san took one look at the fish, which must have weighed at least five kilograms, pursed out his lower lip, and exclaimed, "Oh!"

Bob stood with his back to the wall, threw us a glance, and said, "Mighty big fish."

Some thirty minutes later, Iwabuchi-san was crouched by his fire, cooking up another one of his stews.

"Much too much for this stew. Let's have half of it as sashimi," he said. "Do you think Bob will eat sashimi? I bet he wishes he was back home."

"You talkin' about me?" said Bob.

"Iwabuchi-san is going to make sashimi, raw fish. Is that okay with you?"

"I will eat whatever you do," he said, smiling weakly and turning his eyes to the wall.

We ate dinner in silence, like a family. Only a few words were spoken: "Good?" "Good." "Want more?" "Thank you." "Lot of fish." "Yeah. Can't get any fresher."

After dinner, the three of us dozed off as the fire died out between us. I woke up first in what was almost a pitch-black space. For a moment, I couldn't see a thing. Then, gradually, I could make out the white ash faintly smoldering under the pot. Both Iwabuchi-san and Bob were flat on their backs, dead to the world. I groped my way around the curve into the back room. I had seen Iwabuchi-san take matches from the wooden box next to the archway. I knelt down on the sand and crawled to the box with my right hand out. When I felt the box, I opened its lid and found some matches. I struck a match close to my face.

"Thank you for bringing the fish and vegetables," said Iwabuchi-san, standing in the entrance of the room.

"Oh, I didn't know you were there."

"I just got up. The match is burning down. You'll burn yourself. Here."

I dropped the match. It went out the instant it touched the sand. Again it was pitch-black. Suddenly, Iwabuchi-san's face lit up. He had lit his lighter. He took a short candle from his shirt pocket and thrust its wick into the flame.

"You have been so kind to me. And to Bob. You are so young. Why is such a young girl so full of compassion? Your parents must be remarkable people."

"I don't know."

"Well, most young girls would either run away or turn us in to the military police. If we were turned in, both of us would be executed. You would be considered a hero. Very brave. A model for others. But now you, too, are in danger. I am very grateful to you. You are saving Bob's life. He is not well. Sometimes he is very weak. But now I think you should leave here

71

and never come back. It is too dangerous for you. You may lose your life along with us. Leave us. We are death to you."

I had no answer for Iwabuchi-san. I didn't know myself why I was continuing to go to the cave. I could not see how the three of us could possibly survive the war.

"Can I ask you a question?"

"Yes, Hiromi-san, sure."

"Why are you so concerned about Bob? He's your enemy. Well, maybe not your personal enemy. But right now Americans like him are killing Japanese soldiers and civilians. There is a battle going on now in Okinawa."

"Oh, so the Americans have invaded?"

"Yes."

"When?"

"I don't know. A few days ago, maybe."

"Oh, then . . . it won't be long."

"What won't be long?"

"The end."

"Really?"

The candle flickered. Iwabuchi-san cupped his hand around the flame. This lit up his face more brightly than before.

"Yes. Of course Japan will lose. Next year, maybe, or the year after. Many millions of Japanese people will still have to die before then, though. We brought this all upon ourselves. We deserve our fate, even those of us who resisted it in vain. Many Japanese who are against this war will die in it, and many who love this war will survive it. Maybe that's the biggest tragedy of all."

"So, you didn't answer my question, Iwabuchi-san. About Bob."

"You are very insistent for a young Japanese girl."

"I was brought up in America."

"Ah, well, that explains it. Well, why should I kill him? Bob is not my enemy. He is just like me. We are two frogs, you know, in a very small pond. So long as our pond is not discovered, we will live together happily . . . well, if this here can be called happily. Isn't that what some people call a kind of love? Being left alone to fulfill your life as you see fit in the presence of others you care about, whoever they might be? Once you are brought together with someone, they cannot be ignored or forgotten."

He swung his left arm in a full circle to indicate the space that was now his entire world.

"Love? Why love?" I asked. "What does this have to do with love?"

I don't think I had ever said the word *ai*, love, in Japanese before. In fact, I don't think I had ever mentioned "love" in English either. Takaaki once said it to me, when we were really little. He said that Mom and Dad loved us, and that meant we had to do what we were told.

"Hey, what's goin' on here?" said Bob, now standing behind Iwabuchi-san. "Havin' a powwow?"

Iwabuchi-san turned around and, grinning from one ear to the other, said in English, "Ye-su, ye-su!"

"You see, Iwabuchi-san understands," said Bob. "Iwabuchi-san understands everything."

SAME DAY

NIGHTTIME

CLEAR, STARRY SKY

"Are you sure that this is safe?" I asked Bob.

"You yourself said no one ever comes to this side of the island at night. Anyway, we'll hear someone coming if they do."

Bob and I had left the cave, striding right up to the shoreline. The seaweed was now gone, pulled back into the sea by the tide. The only thing along the shore besides my string bag was a piece of smooth driftwood the size of a large open book.

"Just for a minute or two. We shouldn't stay out here for long. I'll get my star sand, and then I'll go home."

"Okay, sure. Just a moment or two."

Bob stretched, reaching for the sky with both hands.

"Oh my God, this is amazing. What a sky! I've never seen a sky like this, not even at Fort Bliss, where I went to boot camp."

Two black kites circling above the grotto suddenly shot across the beach and disappeared over the island.

"Is that where you're from?"

"What, Fort Bliss? Hell no. That's in Texas. God forbid! I already told you. Bensonhurst."

"Oh yes, I forgot. Sorry."

Our legs were extended in front of us. The waves were just about reaching our toes. A single gull was flying over the sea, rising and falling, as if tossed by the currents of the wind. For a time, Bob seemed lost in its motion.

"He's so nice."

"Who?"

"Iwabuchi-san. Who else would I be talking about?"

Again there was a pause. The breeze coming off the sea was warm. I breathed in twice, deeply.

"Can I hold your hand, Hiromi-san?"

I gave him my hand. He took it between his palms.

"Don't get the wrong idea. I'm not like that."

"Not like what?"

"You know, holding girls' hands an' things."

I smiled at him, and he smiled back.

"I saw a sky like this before, you know, on the ship taking us over here from San Francisco. The Milky Way was like a huge sandbar streaking across the whole big sky. God, sometimes I . . ."

Bob paused again. I could see tears welling in his eyes. He was pressing my hand tightly between his palms.

"You think of home a lot?"

"Yeah. A lot. You know, it's funny the things you remember. I guess the war triggers certain memories. I sort of flashed back now to the parachute jump at

Coney Island, 'cause of the sky, I guess, that bird flyin' up and down."

"Where's that?"

"What, you don't know Coney Island?" he said incredulously, tweaking his nose and sniffling away the tears.

"I was brought up in Los Angeles and Japan."

"Yeah, I guess so. Different world. No, so, they got this parachute-jump ride that Dad made me go on when I was eight. I was terrified. Still am, and now it's for real. But I had to do it, 'cause he said, 'Listen, Bobby, you don't go on that and you'll be a sissy all your life.' So on I go, and the goddamn thing plunged outta the sky just like that, stopping just short of the ground."

"It's just a ride, though, isn't it?"

"Yeah, but to an eight-year-old kid it's the only real thing. I was scared out of my mind. They had to take me home after that, I couldn't stop shaking. Mom read the riot act to Dad, said he was a bully and a tyrant. Poor Dad, he didn't say a word, just took it like a man. Anyway, I remember the day not only because of that, but also 'cause I got to go on the big slide, this enormous high and wide shiny wooden slide, which I went down about a hundred times, even though it squeaks when you go down it and gives you kind-of burns on your elbows an' things, and 'cause I got to eat three portions of cotton candy. You know what that is, don't you?"

"Yes. They have cotton candy in Los Angeles, too."

"Well, I've never been there, but you see everything in the movies, so I guess they got everything."

I stood up, slipping my hand from between Bob's palms.

"Well, the tide's nearly full, and I really ought to go home, and you really ought to get back in the cave. This isn't really a good idea."

"You mean sitting here with you?"

"No. You going out."

Bob rose and handed me my string bag.

"What's in this stuff anyway?"

"What stuff?"

"This stuff you call star sand."

"There's nothing in it. It *is* star sand."

"But what's star sand?"

"It's a tiny marine animal that lives—"

"You mean this stuff you have in these bottles is an animal?"

"Yes. What's left of it after it dies. They are all shaped like stars, tiny little stars. You can keep them for good luck if you want, as your very own little stars."

"Jesus, that's amazing. That's really amazing."

We walked back to the mouth of the cave, where I had left my furoshiki and spear.

"Here, Bob. You take this for yourself," I said, placing a bottle of star sand in his hand and closing his fingers around it.

"But you are going to sell this."

"Who knows . . . but, really, who would ever want this? It has no value."

"It does to me."

Bob closed both hands around the bottle of star sand, and we looked up at the sky.

"Look," I said. "You can see the whole Milky Way. In Japanese it's called 'the River in the Sky.'"

"Amazing. Absolutely amazing," said Bob, shaking his head back and forth.

"Good night, Bob."

"Good night, Hiromi-san."

Before I could move from the spot, Bob dashed back to the shore. He removed the cloth top on the bottle, poured a fistful of star sand into his hand, and threw it way up into the air. I watched as a gust of wind coming off the island carried it out over the sea.

"Hiromi-san, look!" he said, pointing up to the sky. "Your star sand has gone right up to the River in the Sky. It won't come down ever, Hiromi-san. Not ever."

There was a ship on the horizon, but I don't think Bob saw it. He was looking straight up at the white stripe of the Milky Way shining above Hatoma Isle.

I wondered who that ship belonged to. I was a part of both sides, so it had to be mine.

The last thing I saw as I climbed over the rocks was Bob on the shore. He was standing as before, a blur of white, perfectly still in his faded uniform, both his hands, with fingers spread, reaching into the sky.

APRIL 6, 1945

FINE, BUT WINDY

This day changed everything for us on Hatoma Isle.

According to the radio, the fighting in Okinawa was reaching a climax, and the Japanese forces were winning. The people of Okinawa were suffering immeasurably at the brutal hands of the Americans. But thousands of Americans had been killed or captured, and it wouldn't be long before their forces were totally repelled. I had no way to know whether this was the truth or not, but I did believe that a fierce battle was being waged far to the north on the main island of Okinawa.

The cucumbers were now large and bulbous. Had I left them on the vine any longer, they would have been watery and tasteless. I picked the six biggest ones and put them into my furoshiki. The wind was blowing from the south in intermittent warm gusts. I covered my head with a plain cotton scarf and set out to visit the Yoshigami sisters and offer them cucumbers as a neighborly gesture. I had never been to visit them before.

When I arrived at their house not far from the dock, both of them were outside in the front. The elder sister was sitting in the shade of a tall banana tree, weaving a bamboo basket. Just outside the circle of the tree's shade, six turtles lay fastened onto planks, their feet paddling helplessly in the air. A string tied tightly around their heads clamped their jaws shut. The younger sister was sitting with her legs extended on a straw mat beside a lean-to. She was holding a small turtle upside down in her lap. She pulled the belly plate from its body with one forceful tug. The turtle's legs flapped and shuddered, and its blood gushed down into a metal basin between the woman's legs.

"Good morning," I called, standing between two low stone walls at the entrance to the front garden.

The younger sister looked up, the dripping turtle's body still in her hands.

"Oh, good morning. You've come at a good time. This fresh blood is delicious and very nutritious. Used to be my husband's favorite thing to accompany a drink," she said, smiling pleasantly at me.

"I've brought you some cucumbers. They've gotten a bit big, but I think they would still make nice pickles."

I put the furoshiki down beside a flowering hibiscus bush and untied it.

"That's kind of you, Umeno-san," said the younger sister, slicing the flesh out of the shell with a fruit knife. She threw a glance at the furoshiki and grimaced. It was obvious that she was not pleased with this gift of overripe cucumbers. "Did you see the boat come in yesterday?"

"No," I said, covering the cucumbers with a flap of the furoshiki.

"They apparently did some looking around. Apparently, some people have been hoarding animals. Some people seem to think they can get away with it because Hatoma is so isolated. They don't realize that there is no such thing as isolation at a time like this."

"May as well not be a war on as far as we here know, though," said the elder sister, twisting a thin strip of bamboo around the handle of her basket. "The war is somewhere else as far as I'm concerned."

The younger sister tipped the basin to see how much blood was in it.

"Who were they?" I asked.

"Who?"

"The people who came on the boat."

"Oh, the army, of course. They are heading north from Iriomote, first to Miyakojima, then as far as they can get. Only about ten soldiers, I think. We saw them go from the dock up the path there. I greeted one of them, a fine-looking young man who bowed to me very politely and said how anxious he was to go north to fight the enemy."

"Did they find any animals?"

The Yoshigami sisters exchanged glances.

"Uh, we don't know anything about that," said the younger sister. "It's not our business what goes on in other people's lives. Just our own."

"Yes, just our own," repeated the elder sister.

The two sisters resumed their tasks. The younger one wiped her palms with a cloth that was on her lap.

"Well, I'll be getting back now."

"You look after yourself now," she said, peering at me. "My sister here can't do that. Can't look after herself."

"That's not true," said the older sister under her breath.

"What did you say? It is true. You know, she fell down in the kitchen the other day and couldn't get up. I left her there for a whole day, just so that she would know how dependent she really is on me. If I had gone away for good, she would have died. She forgets sometimes where she is."

"Oh, I do not. Not much. Just sometimes. Maybe I ate that thing that makes you forget things."

"What thing?"

"You know, that thing."

"Myoga ginger?"

"Yes, that's it. I always forget what it is."

"So you see, Umeno-san. You have to look after yourself. You cannot rely on anyone to look after you, like my sister here. Good-bye, now. And thank you for the cucumbers. Just leave them there by the hibiscus bush."

The hibiscus flowers on the bush were orange, with a ball of yellow pollen at the end of the stalk in the center of each flower. A bee had flown onto a stalk and buried its head in the pollen. I looked up at the Yoshigami sisters. The elder one was weaving her basket, her bronzed hands deftly twisting, pulling, and securing the thin strips of bamboo. The younger sister had leaned the turtle's gouged-out shell against the side of the house to dry in the sun. She was crouching over the remaining turtles, deciding which one to take next.

I returned to my house, filled the wooden bath with rainwater from the tank under the drainpipe, and lit a fire under the tub with kindling and a bundle of thin branches. Morning was my favorite time to have a bath.

While waiting for the water to heat, which only took fifteen minutes on Hatoma because the water was so warm to begin with, I started steaming two big sweet potatoes that I had cut into chunks, enough for Iwabuchi-san, Bob, and me. When the bath was ready, I sank into the hot water. Sitting in the bath, I could see the tops of the trees in the garden and the oval sky suspended between them. Streaky lines of cloud crisscrossed the oval, like scales on a pale-blue fish. A gust of wind blew through the little window above the bath, rattling the frame and sending the spider weaving a web in the window scurrying into a corner.

I thought about what the Yoshigami sisters had said. "It's not our business what goes on in other people's lives. Just our own." I realized I must only look after my own life. If I myself did not survive, then how would I ever be able to consider others, to care for them, to keep them alive and remembered?

By the time I was out of the bath, the potatoes were half-cooked. I wrapped the pieces in a large banana leaf, rinsed the pot, and set out for the cave.

I arrived at the cave just before noon. The sun was beating down on the beach from directly above me, and the sand was so bright that it hurt my eyes. Seaweed lay, as before, in odd little pyramids about a meter and a half from the shoreline. The water was clear enough to see the seabed all the way to the grotto, where it flowed into the arched openings, dyed dark blue by the shade. Six or seven gulls were coasting over the water but not dipping into it. They suddenly changed direction and headed for shore, and each one took up a space between piles of seaweed. They hunched down and craned their necks, calling out in cornet voices.

I walked along the beach to where the grotto jutted from the rock face into the water. I stretched to get

my head around the jagged corner. It must be somewhere around here, I thought, that the back room of
the cave is joined to the inside of the grotto. I put
my furoshiki down, slipped out of my straw sandals,
and, without cuffing up my mompe, stepped into the
shallow water and ducked under the low arch of the
grotto. I had never before been inside the grotto so
close to shore.

The rock face rose about three meters above
the waterline and then curved around above my
head to form the grotto's ceiling. It was cool and
shady under there, and the water seeping through
the mompe chilled my skin. My arms and the nape
of my neck broke out in goose pimples. I shivered
and brought my upper arms flush against my sides.
This seemed to keep the chill at bay. I relaxed my
right arm and reached up as high as I could, which
wasn't very high, given my height, and swept my
fingers over the sharp-edged rocks. Close to the far
edge of the rock face was a crevice that ran up to the
ceiling. There was nothing to stand on, so I couldn't
tell if this was the same crevice as the one in the
back room of the cave.

Then, I heard a voice coming from the crevice.
It was a shouting voice, in Japanese. But because
of the sound of the water lapping against the rocks
and because my ear was a meter below the crevice, I
could not make out the words. I could tell only that

they were being spoken in anger. I stood as still as I could, leaning against the rocks, not budging. The voice stopped, and there was silence. Then the voice continued again, bellowing more gruffly than before. Yet, no matter how still I remained, I could not make out the words.

I left the grotto, wrung my cuffs and shook my legs, slapped my shirt to rid it of excess water, put my sandals back on, picked up my furoshiki, and entered the cave. I knocked twice on the driftwood door with a stone. The door opened. Standing in the doorway was Iwabuchi-san's uncle.

"Come in," he said. "I've heard that you have been coming here."

I entered the cave. He shut the door behind me. Several candles lit the room. Iwabuchi-san was there, next to the rectangular area on the wall that he had polished until it shone . . . and another man. The other man was dressed in what looked like a white hospital robe. The robe was untied. I could see his loincloth and naked torso. He stood with a crutch under his armpit. His left leg below the knee was covered in a coffee-colored cast. Bob was nowhere to be seen.

The man with the crutch and Iwabuchi-san were staring at each other with blank expressions. I turned to the uncle. His eyes were fixed straight ahead, as if peering right through the two men.

"Is this the girl?" said the man with the crutch.

"Yes," said Iwabuchi-san.

"Is that all the people you are harboring here?"

Just then I saw Bob coming out of the room that Iwabuchi-san called the inner sanctum, rounding the corner on the path to the main room. Iwabuchi-san's expression rapidly changed. He could obviously tell from the frightened look on my face that I had seen Bob.

The man with the crutch swiveled around. He immediately thrust out his crutch like a rifle and pointed it at Bob, supporting himself with his left arm against the wall.

"Stop! Stop there!" he hollered.

Bob stopped in his tracks.

"Put your hands up!"

Bob put both of his hands in the air.

"Stay where you are!"

"I'm not going anywhere, you can be sure of that," said Bob, though it appeared that I was the only one in the room who understood him.

"Shut up!"

Bob tried to put his index finger to his lips to indicate that he would not speak, but the man raised his crutch again. Bob nodded and held both hands straight up over his head.

"Who is this man? He is American."

"Yes, *aniki*, he is."

"What are you doing here with him, eh? He must be turned in to the army and dealt with properly. What are you all doing here, eh? My younger brother, a deserter. An enemy soldier. A girl who is probably a spy. And an uncle who is providing food and shelter for all of you. Who's the crazy one here, eh? You're all crazy, that's who! Cowards, all of you! Traitors! You don't deserve to live."

"Can you please ask the man to let me put my arms down," said Bob. "They're hurting. Tell him that I wouldn't do anything in a million years."

I translated what Bob said.

"He's absolutely harmless, *aniki*," said Iwabuchi-san. "He's also very weak. He has dysentery now."

This other man, then, was Iwabuchi-san's elder brother.

For a moment the brother didn't move. He scrutinized the four of us with an expression of utter disgust. He abruptly jerked his crutch downward. Bob lowered his arms and rubbed his muscles.

"Boy," he said, "I didn't realize how hard it is just to surrender. Can I go past here, please?"

The elder brother must have picked up Bob's meaning from his imploring facial expression and his outstretched palm. With a swing of his crutch he indicated for Bob to enter the room.

"Excuse me, please," he said, walking past the brother.

"I should have you all arrested and put away. Damn boat has left, though. You will not survive this, I promise you. When Japan wins the war, you will know what real suffering is. Family means nothing."

"I'm sorry," said Bob to me. "I was in the john. Who are these two men, Hiromi-san?"

"This is Iwabuchi-san's *aniki*, his elder brother. This is his uncle, also Iwabuchi-san."

"How do you do? How do you do?" said Bob to each man. "I'm sorry not to offer you my hand, but I just got out of the john and . . ."

Iwabuchi-san's uncle bowed. His brother turned his face away and spit into the sand.

"You didn't tell me about your a-nee-kee, Iwabuchi-san. Is that how you pronounce it? He didn't tell me, Hiromi-san. Did he get that injury in battle? I am so sorry. Really so sorry. Please tell him that."

I translated what Bob said, and again the brother turned his face to one side and spit into the sand.

"Hajime was injured two years ago at Guadalcanal. When he recovered, he insisted on not going home. They sent him to the Philippines, but he injured his leg when evacuating Palawan Island and was brought here yesterday by boat, seeing as I am his uncle. He really can't walk very well. You will have to look after him here for a while, just until his knee improves."

"But why don't you look after him, Uncle?"

"I have to leave Hatoma now, maybe as early as tomorrow. I've got a boat. I'm going to Hateruma or Yonaguni to wait out the war. It won't be long now. Over by the new year, I'd say. I can't stay. I'm sorry."

"Yes, and when it's over . . . ," said the elder brother, digging the tip of his crutch into the sand where his spit had fallen, ". . . when it's over, we will come looking for you. Family doesn't matter. His Majesty the Emperor is the sole family of all Japanese."

Bob, visibly feeble on his feet from his dysentery, approached the elder brother.

"I am sorry, a-nee-kee-san. Please forgive me and my people. We did not want to do this to you."

I translated what he said.

"I understand it. It is meaningless. He is the enemy. You are all the enemy!"

He twisted his crutch, digging the end of it more deeply into the little wet pit by his feet.

"Why do you have to leave, Uncle? If you do, we will have no one to provide everything we need . . . the candles, matches, rice, water when it doesn't rain."

"This young girl will have to provide everything from now on. I cannot stay. When the soldiers delivered your brother to my home yesterday, they noticed my water buffalo and my goat. I was not supposed to keep these. They took the water buffalo with them on the boat and slaughtered my goat right in front of me. They made me cook it up for them and ate a hearty meal. I had some leftovers. I put them over there, in the corner. Eat them today, and they will still be fresh. The officer said that if there wasn't a battle in Okinawa now, they would take me like they took the water buffalo and put me in jail on Ishigaki. But for now I would just slow them down, so they let me stay. But they promised to send soldiers from Ishigaki to get me. I must leave. I may leave tonight. It's safe to sail at night. I can make it to one of the islands by sometime tomorrow. I will be safe, don't worry about me. If you remain here, you, too, will be safe until this is all over."

"They will not be safe!" shouted the elder brother. "The moment I can walk out of here by myself, that will be the end of three traitors at once. Cowards! Traitors! Cowards!" he repeated, now using his crutch to pound the sand.

The uncle bowed individually to each of us, opened the door, and left, shutting it behind him. The four of us remained in our places without saying a word. Finally, Iwabuchi-san broke the silence.

"*Aniki*," he said, "have something to eat anyway. Let's have lunch now. The goat will be best if eaten fresh."

The elder brother put his crutch under his armpit and hobbled into a corner. Iwabuchi-san served a portion of goat meat to him, another portion to Bob, and one to me. There were only three plates in the cave.

Iwabuchi-san ate his goat off the banana leaf that it was wrapped in.

"Oh, too much for me, Iwabuchi-san," said Bob, holding the plate in front of him. "Please give half of this to a-nee-kee-san."

"Iran!" ("Keep it!") said the elder brother, turning his back to us and facing the wall.

Not long after, he fell asleep, breathing regularly with his mouth open, slumped in front of the wall with his crutch propped against his neck.

"I feel so sorry for your a-nee-kee, Iwabuchi-san," said Bob, putting his plate on a plank in the sand. "Please tell him that, Hiromi-san. He must be in a lot of pain. Pain surely makes you angry. I know that. I mean, I saw so much of it. Those guys I fought with stopped caring about themselves. All they wanted to do was inflict the same pain on men on the other side. Their own lives came to mean nothing to them."

I translated this for Iwabuchi-san.

"I understand," said Iwabuchi-san. "It is terrible that he has been injured like that. I think that this has only made him more convinced that Japan will win this war."

I translated this for Bob. Bob simply shrugged his shoulders, as if he didn't know which side would win and the outcome was of no concern to him anymore. Then, all of a sudden, he said, "Uh-oh," gripped his belly, and rushed out to the inner sanctum.

"Bob is not well. I am terribly worried about him," said Iwabuchi-san.

"He needs rest and good food. I will have to find as much food for you and him as I can. I will take over for your uncle. There is no need for you to leave this cave, ever."

"Hiromi-san, you are an angel."

"Really? I am not. I am no angel, Iwabuchi-san. I only think of what to do as each day arrives. When I listen to the radio, I don't think about how what I've heard will affect the future. For me the future is this evening, tonight, and maybe as late as tomorrow morning. Whatever happens after that, I don't see as being connected with me."

Iwabuchi-san stood up and approached me. He crouched beside me, then whispered:

"Hiromi-san. You must live. *You* must survive this. Only you can tell people what happened."

"You and Bob and your elder brother and your uncle and everyone must survive this, too, Iwabuchi-san. It doesn't matter which side—"

"No, shhh," he said, putting his index finger up to my lips, nearly touching them. "Shhh. My brother and I were trained very well. Inside us there is a message, a voice, repeating itself over and over again here, somewhere in our ear or brain. It tells us that our country is the only important thing in the world, more important than family, than friendship, than love itself. Of course, every Japanese knows in his heart that this is not so. But the message is loud, Hiromi-san, and insistent. It doesn't stop. It drowns out every other voice. We cannot shut it off. We know it is not true, but we have no breathing space to think anything else. The message repeats itself with every breath we take, minute by minute, day by day, it chokes us. This cave, with its awful, foul air, its uniform gray darkness, and its black walls . . . this cave has that breathing space. Yes, these walls breathe, Hiromi-san! They have life, and while in here we can continue to live out our lives. Yet, there is no knowing how long we will have here before even this gray light goes out and all the air is sucked out. At that time, the walls, too, will die and take us with them. You can leave here. You *can* survive. You are the lucky one among us, Hiromi-san, the only one who has not hurt another person, the one whose future will last longer than that tomorrow you speak of."

"That is, if anyone at all survives this war. Maybe all Japanese people will perish. Maybe there will be nothing left of this country at all except the mountains, the rivers, the rocks, and the sea."

Iwabuchi-san shook his head back and forth.

"Never. You know, someday, soon, this is all bound to be over. This cave will be sealed and no one will ever bother to look inside. People will be born who look at the mountains, the trees, and the sea with the same wonder that we did. Life goes on, just not one's own. The vital thing is to look after those who come into your reach while you are still alive, good people, bad people, all people. And that is why I am very grateful to you, Hiromi-san. You will go to my uncle's house first thing in the morning and get rice, candles, matches, and medicine, because my brother has a fever. He is not well at all, and he doesn't know what he is saying. He is not himself. I must bring him back. And you must go for Bob, too. Bob swings from being robust to being feeble. Sometimes I think he's half-dead. We must keep them both alive until this war ends. They will become friends, and like all other people will be able to see ahead, to see the future, not just a day or two but a year ahead, a decade ahead, for as long as their lives last."

I nodded, stood, and left the cave. Iwabuchi-san smiled and waved at me from the half-open door, calling to me as I reached the mouth of the outer cave.

"Sorry for the sermon!"

I walked along the beach. The wind had subsided, and the air was calm. The moon hung like a hook above the horizon, and above it, the Milky Way looked like a gauze robe, rolled up and stretched across the sky. When I came to the rocks and began to climb over them toward the path to the southern part of the island, a turtle emerged from the surf, waddling her way up the beach and into the shrubs. I cautiously negotiated my way among the rocks and stood perfectly still some meters from the wall of shrubs.

On a patch of sand in the shrubs, the turtle was digging a hole with her hind legs. I waited. I looked up at the sky and out to the water. Thanks to the moonlight, the surface of the sea was a mosaic of silver and black with shifting lines, one instant straight, the next diagonal or broken into myriad angles.

In a flash, two white figures dashed from the rock cliff toward the shoreline. It was Iwabuchi-san and Bob . . . and they were stark naked! Their bodies glowed, two white blurs racing over the sand into the surf, a moment later fragmenting the lines of light on the angled water and disappearing into it. Then both their heads appeared some distance out, bobbing like ping-pong balls on the silvery surface under the moon.

I gazed down at the turtle. She had now dug a considerably larger hole and partially refilled it with sand, and she was walking away from it without laying any eggs. I had heard that turtles did this in order to trick the birds that would come to feed on their eggs. The turtle began to dig another hole some distance from the first. I could see only her back legs from where I was. The turtle was paddling frantically, kicking sand high into the air behind her. I knew that if I disturbed her, she would be gripped by fear, abandon the pit, and return to the sea without laying her eggs.

I looked back at the sea. Bob was now standing waist-deep in the water, looking around. Iwabuchi-san was nowhere to be seen. The moonlight lit up Bob's face clearly, and he stared for a minute in my direction. But he seemed too alarmed to notice me standing on the rocks. He was obviously worried about Iwabuchi-san, who had not reappeared, but he could not cry out for fear of being discovered.

Some seconds later, I caught sight of Iwabuchi-san's head in the grotto. The head floated toward Bob, who was looking the other way. All of a sudden, Iwabuchi-san jumped out of the water and grabbed Bob by the shoulders. This obviously scared the living daylights out of Bob, who opened his mouth wide in a silent scream. Soon both men were laughing, covering their mouths with their hands.

"Good evening," came a voice from the other side of the rocks.

It was the younger Yoshigami sister. I was instantly overcome by fear, terrified that she would see Iwabuchi-san and Bob. I also threw a quick glance at the turtle. I could not see her, but I was scared that, if she discovered the turtle, the Yoshigami sister would pick her up and carry her home.

"Oh, hello," I said, stepping up to stand between her and the beach. "I was just . . ."

"Star sand, is it?"

"Yes. But—"

"Any turtles here? Did you see any turtles? This is the time of night they usually come ashore to lay their eggs. They used to come up at Yarahama, but they've stopped for some reason. Must be the war. The war changes everything. There's a lot of star sand there, too, by the way. Why don't you go there to get it? It's closer to your home."

She was climbing up to the top of the rocks. In a few seconds she would be high enough to see Iwabuchi-san and Bob, who were now wading through the shallow water toward shore.

"Oh, I know. I do go there, too. But, wait, Yoshigami-san. The reason, I mean, what happened was I started to feel faint, and I had to sit down on the rocks here. I left my star sand back there."

"I'll go get it for you," she said, momentarily losing her balance on a wobbly rock.

"Oh, careful. No, I'll go back for it tomorrow. Could you please help me? I am feeling dizzy. Wait there, please. Wait!"

I looked back at the beach. The two men were now walking across it toward the mouth of the cave. They appeared as a single hazy white figure gliding along the sand. I could not see the turtle laying her eggs among the shrubs. I stepped down toward Yoshigami-san.

"I just lost my balance," she said, standing erect. "I'll come to you."

"No. You mustn't come here at night, Yoshigami-san. It's too dangerous. I mean, these rocks. Here, you take my hand, and I'll take yours. We can help each other down. The rocks are easier to walk over closer to shore."

We held hands and stepped down the rocks onto the sand on the other side.

"Funny to be helping a young girl like you. But I suppose anyone can get sick at any age. And it is that age now for you, isn't it, the age when young women feel, well, under the weather once a month?"

"Oh yes. Thank you. You are so kind."

We walked down the path toward the southern end of the island, Yoshigami-san glancing at me from time to time with an expression of deep care and even, it seemed to me, affection.

APRIL 7, 1945

FINE, LATER SHOWERY
RAIN

I slept much later than usual. The events in the cave the previous day must have tired me out. I have never been good at dealing with conflict. Rather than defend myself or attack the other person, I simply withdraw into myself and sulk, rehearsing in my mind, often with hand gestures and whispered words, arguments on both sides of the conflict. This unnerved my father, who was fond of an argument, even for its own sake. He took one side and stuck to it until the other side capitulated. If it looked as if reason was working against him, he simply changed the subject on you.

I dressed, left the house without eating breakfast, and headed to Iwabuchi-san's uncle's house. I was hoping that he would still be there and that he would give me some provisions and medicine to take to the cave.

The garcinia tree in the front garden could be seen from far down the path, this tree that had withstood typhoons and storms for decades. The wall of jagged, notched stones around the house was higher than the walls around other houses on Hatoma. I turned into the front garden and noticed immediately that the door to the house was open. I stood under the eaves.

"Excuse me," I said. I repeated this more loudly. There was no reply. I stepped into the spacious entryway. The first thing that caught my eye was a chair on its side in the living room. "Excuse me. Iwabuchi-san," I called. I slipped out of my sandals and stepped up into the house. Without warning, Iwabuchi-san's cat jumped out of the living room and ran past me. My right hand flew to my neck, and I exclaimed in English, "Oh my God!"

The living room had an upright piano in one corner and a cabinet housing a record player in another. Several oil paintings in ornate frames hung on the walls, all of them of mountains, some covered in snow. A long built-in bookshelf lined one of the walls. I could see tall books in it about mountain climbing, most of them in English: *Conquering the Alps for Sport and Pleasure* and *The Himalayas: Challenge for the 20th Century*. I wondered why someone so keen on mountain climbing would come to live on this little island, less than one square kilometer in size, at the bottom of a chain of islands leading from Okinawa to Formosa. He was displaced, that's why, I thought. We were all displaced now, perhaps me more than anyone.

There were three framed photographs in front of some books. One was of Iwabuchi-san's uncle as a young man and a pretty woman in a ski sweater. The second must have been a wedding photo, because both of them, unsmiling, were in formal kimonos, the uncle standing and the woman sitting primly beside him. The third photograph showed a family of four on a snowy mountainside. The photograph was out of focus, but it must have been one of the uncle, his wife, and their son and daughter. The four were arm in arm, beaming at the camera. I picked up the frame and turned it around. Written on the back of the photograph was:

At Nagano   1936.12.25

I went into the kitchen and opened a tall cupboard. Iwabuchi-san's uncle was no doubt on his way to Hateruma or Yonaguni. I was sure that he wouldn't mind my coming here on my own and taking food and necessities to the cave, something he had done since Iwabuchi-san went into hiding.

I easily found candles, matches, and the rice, which was in small straw rice bags. I put one bag of rice, a big handful of candles, and several boxes of matches in an empty crate that was under the kitchen table. I planned to wrap the crate in my furoshiki and tie it to my back. But where did he keep his medicines? I searched every room but could not find his first-aid box, the one with a red cross on it that every Japanese family kept. Perhaps, I thought, he took it with him. That would surely make sense.

The pantry at the back of the house was narrow, like a large, open closet. It seemed to be the place where the uncle stored things. There were bottles of Kikkoman soy sauce on the shelves, as well as powdered miso, sugar, salt, little cans of mandarin oranges, and Meiji fruit candy. I stood on my tiptoes and lowered a large, round, unlabeled can from one of the top shelves. I shook it, and it rattled. I tried to pry open the lid of the can, but it wouldn't come off. I took a sharp knife from a box of utensils on the lowest shelf and inserted the blade between the lid and the side of the can, pushing up with all my strength. The lid popped open. Inside were what looked like hard cookies wrapped in cellophane. There was also a small muslin bag of the cookies in the can, and on it was the word *kanpan*. What was kanpan? I had never heard of it. I knelt down, spilled four or five of the cookies onto the floor by my feet, and picked one up, putting it into my mouth and biting down hard with my molars. Just then, a gruff male voice shot out from the entryway.

"Iwabuchi! Iwabuchi, dete koi!" ("Iwabuchi! Show yourself, Iwabuchi!")

I realized instantly that this was the military police. They must have come by boat from Ishigaki. Iwabuchi-san's uncle had been right. He had needed to leave as soon as possible.

I heard the military police tramping through the house. They weren't saying a word to each other. The same cat as before, a tortoiseshell, streaked through the back room and disappeared out the back door. I was frozen to the spot in the pantry, kneeling in front of the shelves with a knife in my hand and half a cookie in my mouth. I crawled backward to a cramped little space between the shelf and the wall and stood up in it, pressing my back against the wall and pulling my feet in as far as they would go. I could not see the door, so perhaps they would not find me unless they entered the room and began examining the shelves. I stared at the cookies on the floor and hoped they would think that Iwabuchi-san's uncle had left them there in his haste to escape.

I could not tell how many soldiers there were, but it seemed like three. Each one was now in a different room. The footsteps of one of them stopped at the door to the pantry. I could hear the soldier turn into the room and walk along the shelves. I caught sight of the barrel of the gun he was pointing in front of him.

"Oi! Koko ni mo oran zo!" ("Hey! No one here either!") he shouted.

Just then the soldier took another step. He was standing in front of me, pointing the gun at my chest. I dropped the knife.

"Heeh," ("Well, well,") he said. Then he shouted out of the side of his mouth, *"Oi! Hayaku koi!"* ("Hey! Come quick!")

Two other soldiers ran into the room. Now all three were standing in front of me.

"Please forgive me. I came to see Iwabuchi-san to get some medicine from him because I am not well, and I don't know where he is. Then I found these cookies and I've been starving, so I started to eat one. I opened the can with the knife and spilled the cookies. I'm sorry."

I started to cry, out of both fear and self-pity. But somewhere deep inside, I must have felt that a young girl's tears might be her only defense before three soldiers. When I was a little girl, I realized that letting the tragic actress inside me out from time to time was the best way to get what I wanted.

One of the other soldiers picked up the knife and weighed it in his hand, leering at me.

"Omae, Iwabuchi no shinseki ka?" ("You a relative of Iwabuchi?") he said.

"Iie. Shirimasen wa," ("No. I don't know him,") I said, half choking on my tears and wiping my nose on my sleeve.

The third soldier crouched down and picked up the cookies. He handed them to me.

"Arigato gozaimasu," ("Thank you very much,") I said.

The soldier with the gun ordered the other two to find the medicine box for me. In a matter of less than a minute it had been located in a futon closet.

The three men discussed Iwabuchi-san's uncle, coming to the conclusion that he had escaped the island, probably leaving in the middle of the night. The man with the gun, who was an officer, said, *"Shikata nee,"* ("Nothin' more we can do here,") and the other two left. I was standing in the living room. The officer pivoted on his heel and ran out. The house was once again deserted and still. I dropped down into a heap on the floor and wept uncontrollably. This time no inner actress was needed to urge me on.

I wept for some minutes and then stopped abruptly. I inhaled deeply, stood, and opened the medicine box that the soldiers had put on the living room table. Inside were a variety of powders and creams and several little seaweed-brown bottles with liquid in them. Though I'd had a few weeks of training as a nurse's aide, I could not identify the nature of the medicines. Iwabuchi-san was sure to know what they were, however. He had been a soldier in the field. I put the medicines in the crate, together with the rice, candles, and matches; slipped on my sandals; and carried the crate all the way home, where I had left my furoshiki.

I entered the house, leaving the crate on the raised floor of the entryway. There was a small purple furoshiki decorated in pink plum blossoms sitting right inside the sliding door of the front room. Next to it was a note:

This is for you, Hiromi-san. We hope that it will make you better soon. Yoshigami sisters

I carefully untied the knot on top of the furoshiki. Inside were six eggs fastened in a row, with straw wrapped around each egg and a loop at the top to carry them. Next to the eggs were three fillet-blocks of dried bonito, which could be used to make shavings for stock. There was an abandoned factory for producing dried bonito on Hatoma, and its soot-stained chimney was still the tallest structure on the island. The sisters must have hoarded these blocks from the time the factory was in operation. I put my hands together and bowed my head, and then I retied the furoshiki and placed it in the crate.

Did the sisters know, I wondered, that there were men harbored in the cave and that I was visiting them? No, they couldn't have known; otherwise, knowing them and their nosy ways, they would have made some reference to it. They might have turned us all in to the military police. The eggs and dried bonito blocks must have been meant for me alone.

Later that day I would go to the cave with the food, medicines, candles, and matches. This would be sure to cheer up Iwabuchi-san, Bob, and Iwabuchi-san's brother. If this wouldn't make them feel content at a time like this, I didn't know what else I could do. But for now, I had to do my washing.

I filled the bath, heated the water, and took a long soak, using a bran bag as soap. I hadn't seen real soap in over a year. I washed all of my clothes in the tub, hanging them over branches of trees and bushes in my garden to dry. I would wait an hour or two until they were dry and then set out for the cave. In the meantime, I was truly starving. I reached into my mompe pocket for the kanpan cookies that had fallen on the floor in Iwabuchi-san's uncle's house and ate them one by one. It took me quite a long time to break them up in my mouth and chew them, but in the end, I felt quite full. I wondered how much longer people would continue to make and eat kanpan. If nothing else, the kanpan in the can would certainly outlast this war and even last to feed people in the next one.

I must have dozed off beside the entryway. I was awakened by the sound of rain on the roof. I dashed into the garden and gathered my shirts; scarves;

underclothes, including my bleached cotton under-garment cloth; and towels, rushing from branch to branch and piling it all over my left arm. A heavy shower was now falling out of a sunny sky. I couldn't tell where the rain was coming from. There wasn't a cloud to be seen. A double rainbow arced over the island. The raindrops were like glass beads gleaming in the air.

I was wary of taking such a beautiful scene as a sign of anything, particularly of good fortune or hope. I was not allowing myself anything resem-bling hope. No landscape, no flower, no sea or sky or meadow could be that beautiful in wartime. Getting through each day required ignoring the beauty around me. Making sure that those I was in contact with survived that day was my sole aspira-tion. Hope would no more make it realizable than its dark sister, prayer . . . and I wouldn't be caught dead praying.

The younger Yoshigami sister had, by coinci-dence, been right. My period had started while I was dozing, and lines of blood had seeped through the crotch of my mompe. I washed them out with water. This was my first period in eighteen months. I had thought that they had ceased for good.

I felt a series of sharp pains in my lower belly, like pangs of hunger. I wrapped my freshly washed bleached cotton cloth around my hips. It was still slightly damp from the rain, but that didn't bother me. I boiled some water and made myself a pot of jasmine tea. While it was brewing, I untied the purple furoshiki and managed to slip an egg out of its straw wrapping. I cracked the egg over the sink and ate it raw from the shell, one half at a time. It slid smoothly down my throat. I barely tasted it. But when I licked my lips, the tip of my tongue was coated in thick, sweet yolk. I drank two cups of tea in succession, burning the roof of my mouth. The perfumed scent of the jasmine steam filled my nostrils. I closed my eyes, breathing in the steam and licking my lips over and over again for any part of the egg that might still be on them.

The pain in my belly had subsided. I pulled my mompe down and loosened the cloth, examining the inside of my underpants. There were only a few spots of blood on them. The flow had stopped.

I laid my large furoshiki on the floor of the living room and flattened out its four corners with my palms. I put the crate in the middle, covering it with the small purple furoshiki decorated in plum blossoms; wrapped the crate in my furoshiki; knelt down on one knee; and lifted it onto my back. I tied the four corners of the furoshiki in front of my chest and, bending forward, hoisted it higher up my back. I shuffled my way to the entryway, turned carefully, and looked back into the house to check if I had forgotten something. I could not think of anything. When I turned toward the front door again, a woman was standing in it.

"Oh, hello," I said.

"Who are you?"

"Um, I'm Umeno Hiromi."

"What are you doing here?" She glanced past me into the house.

"I'm, um, living here. This is my, I mean, where I . . ."

"This is my home."

She walked past me, kicking off her shoes as she entered and surveying the house to see if anything was missing.

"Are you Mrs. Gima?"

"Yes. This is my home."

"Oh. I am so sorry," I said, untying and lowering the furoshiki to the ground with a twist of my back. "I came to live here because, well, it was empty, I mean, I thought I could look after the house, and the Yoshigami sisters said it would be all right."

"What right do they have to give such permission?"

She stepped out of the living room into the kitchen. I followed her.

"Everything is here. I have not used, I mean, taken anything that, I mean, of yours."

She didn't say a word as she walked from room to room, inspecting walls, furniture, boxes, everything, with squinted eyes.

"Well, I am back now, so you can leave."

"But . . ."

That was all I could say. I simply stood in front of her in the back room, staring blankly at her. I felt like crying again, but no tears would come out. She pulled the rake out of the crate beside the radio.

"Oh, I've used some of your tools. There are sweet potatoes, uh, vegetables in the garden. Please have them."

Again she remained silent, this time looking me up and down.

"How old are you?"

"Sixteen. Well, nearly seventeen."

"Alone?"

"Pardon?"

"Are you alone?"

"Yes."

"Where are your parents?"

"They're, um, not here, because, I mean, of the war. My father's in Nagasaki, I think. At least that's—"

"I went through Nagasaki last week."

She turned around and stood by the window that looked south. A small patch of sea was visible through the trees that marked the boundary of her property.

"I was told that you were in Osaka?"

"That's correct," she said curtly, keeping her back to me.

"Did you just come from Osaka, or . . . ?"

"Yes."

She slowly turned toward me, leaning her back against the sill.

"You can stay here for a while, if you wish."

"Oh, but I would be a burden to you."

"My daughter was older than you," she said, tightly pursing her lips. "She . . ."

"I'm sorry."

"She was twenty, just. A bit more than three weeks ago, we were living together near Tennoji in Osaka. The bombs came at night, a shower of fire everywhere you looked, and when the fire struck one place, it jumped like this." She swung her arm in an arc, then brought it down from place to place. "First here, then there, here and there, here and there, a cliff of fire, all rushing toward you, one cliff, then another, then another, then another and another."

She was sweeping her arm back and forth, up and down, more and more frantically. Suddenly, she held her arm still in midair.

"We both ran out of the house when it was set ablaze. Within seconds it was an inferno. But the alleyways around Tennoji are narrow, and the houses are all made of wood, so there was nowhere we could run. Then a high wall of fire, like a huge wave, started rolling toward us. It was rolling with its bottom churning up within itself. I jumped into a doorway. It was high and concrete, it must have been some sort of official building or something, I had never seen it before, I didn't know where we were, and my daughter, who was ahead of me, turned and looked back. For an instant, I think, she could see me. But by then it was too late. The wave of fire crashed into her, and I saw her being engulfed in flames. She called out to me, screaming *'Okaasan!'* ('Mom!'), falling to her knees, writhing, with fire shooting out of her body in front and back, and with her hair forced up by the wind, which was itself made of flames, red and bright-yellow flames streaming straight out of her head. She fell backward into the fire and vanished, like a body being taken by the sea. I stood in the concrete doorway until the wave passed me by. By the time I got to her, her body was a pile of charred chunks. It had fallen apart. Even her bones were black and smoking. I picked this up and just continued to walk, down streets, along a river, more streets . . . then in a truck and on a train. The last two weeks have been a blur. People have been kind to me, helped me. A man in Nagasaki had a fishing boat. He was from Ishigaki. How he managed to get it out of the harbor at night, with all the patrols, and south to Ishigaki, is a miracle. We stopped one night on Miyakojima. There were soldiers there, soldiers everywhere. He let me off at the Hatoma dock about half an hour ago."

When Mrs. Gima had said, "I picked this up and continued to walk," she had put her hand in her jacket pocket. Now she took it out and opened her fist. In it was a charred, stringy, glue-like substance. Soot from it had rubbed off on her palm, turning it pitch-black.

"This is Hitomi's hair. It came off her head without any effort, like a clump of buckwheat noodles . . . like . . ."

She closed her fist on the charred hair and clenched it tightly, clamping her lips together to hold back tears.

"I'm sorry."

"They did this to us. The enemy. And they dropped leaflets telling us to surrender, telling us that the war was lost, telling us that we are only prolonging our own agony. They are murderers. They are animals, not humans. Murderers. All cold-blooded murderers! Down to the last man, woman, and child."

She clenched her fist more tightly, and then she relaxed it and carefully placed her daughter's hair back in her pocket, staring past me with vacant, tear-filled eyes toward the vegetable garden on the north side of the house. She reached for the rake without looking down, grasped its handle, and walked by me, stepping right onto the narrow, splintered veranda and into the garden, where she began raking bare soil.

I could not stay with her. She would ask me for more details about my family, and I would tell her that my mother and brother were Japanese Americans, like me, and that I had spent most of my childhood in California. That would make me a murderer, or at least half a murderer. I would be her daughter's murderer by virtue of who my mother was and where I was born.

I decided then and there to ask Iwabuchi-san's permission to live in his uncle's house. I figured that neither his uncle nor the military police would be returning there.

I stood by the veranda and looked out at the Gimas' garden.

"Well, good-bye, Mrs. Gima," I said. "I am so sorry."

She didn't raise her head. She just continued to rake invisible leaves into a single spot.

I went back to the entryway, hoisted the furoshiki with the crate onto my back, slipped into my sandals, and set out for the cave. While on the path going to the north side of the island, I looked up at the sky.

Black and white clouds alternated across it like piano keys. From the high point of the island I could see that rain was falling in a number of places all around it, forming miniature rainbows that hung in the air like little hats, vanished, and then reappeared some distance away.

I was nearly running by the time I reached the rocky point. I had not noticed the colors of the hibiscus flowers bordering the path down to the point. I didn't stop to think about the smoothness of the sea's surface. I set my eye on the black mouth of the cave alone and my mind on its inner cavern, where three men would be waiting for me to arrive with what they needed to survive this day. If I could focus on that and that alone, I might be able to survive myself.

"Bob and I have been worried about you," said Iwabuchi-san, letting me in.

"I'm sorry for not coming earlier. You must be very hungry."

"We haven't eaten today, but we're all right—except for my brother. He has been delirious since last night. Must be the fever."

"Oh," I said, looking over his shoulder at his brother, who was slumped in a sitting position like a rag doll propped up against the wall.

"Bob has been looking after him."

Bob, who was sitting with his legs crossed in front of what was now a small polished circle in the wall by the door, spun his head around.

"Hullo," he said in a high-pitched child's voice, before turning once more to the wall.

Even though the rains had stopped, water was dripping from the opening in the dome into the pail below. The drip of the water was loud and regular, like the ticking of a clock. Iwabuchi-san's brother opened his eyes wide and stared at us, but then closed them just as suddenly.

"Did you see my uncle?"

"No, Iwabuchi-san. He must have left in the middle of the night. I went to his home to get these things. Can I put them down?"

"Oh, sorry. They must be very heavy. Here."

He lifted the furoshiki off my back and placed it carefully on the ground by the pail. Bob turned his head ever so slightly, throwing a glance at the furoshiki through the corner of his eye before returning to his wall.

"Thank you," I said. "There's some food in there from the Yoshigami sisters, too."

"They don't know we're here, do they?" he said with some alarm.

"No. No, they don't. They gave me the food because I told them I was ill."

"You're not, are you?"

"No. No. Of course not. I'm fine."

I was going to tell Iwabuchi-san about the military police, but I decided that this might only further alarm him. He untied the furoshiki, laying the ends on the ground, and removed the small purple furoshiki covering the crate's contents.

"Oh, dried bonito. How wonderful! This will make our soups taste so much better. What a godsend this is, real dried bonito at a time like this. Look, Bob."

Bob, who naturally had not understood a word, turned toward us.

"Hey, amazing. Wood is it, for the fire?"

Bob had mistaken the dried blocks of bonito for small logs of wood.

"It's dried fish, for the soup," I explained.

"Amazing," he said, nodding and digging his behind deep into the sand, sitting with his back perfectly straight in front of his wall.

"There's some medicine in the box, but I don't really know what it's for."

"I'll work it out," said Iwabuchi-san. "You just rest. I can see that you have had a trying day already. It must be very hard for you, Hiromi-san, having three desperate men on your hands."

I was going to say, "No, not at all," but I knew that this would not convince Iwabuchi-san. Like all young girls, I was good at lying, but only about objective things, not when it came to talking about my emotional state.

Iwabuchi-san began to unpack the food, medicine, candles, and matches. Each item was greeted with a grunt of approval. I went to his brother and knelt by his side. As if hearing me kneeling beside him, he jerked himself away from the wall.

"What are you doing here?" he said, staring at me with contempt. "Don't you dare touch me, do you hear?"

"Shh, *aniki*," said Iwabuchi-san, shaving some dried bonito into a metal bowl with a sharp knife. "Go back to sleep. We've got medicine for you now, and look, dried bonito. Just like Mother used to use. You'll be fit as a fiddle before you know it."

"I don't want her looking after me, medicine or no medicine," he said. "I wish you were all dead."

"She won't be," said Iwabuchi-san. "I'm looking after you. Don't worry. Now, sit back against the wall and get your rest."

Once again the brother glared spitefully, this time at the three of us, gradually closing his lids and easing back until his head bumped against the wall. It was then that I noticed he was holding Bob's gun in both hands over his chest. I looked at Iwabuchi-san, indicating the gun by cocking my head once toward it.

"It's all right. It doesn't work. He cleaned it and tried to fix it, but it's beyond repair. Bob knew what he was doing. My brother feels better holding it over his heart. It calms him."

Iwabuchi-san lit a fire under the pot. About a third of the water that had been in the pail was now in the pot, and shavings of dried bonito were waving on top of the water as if being blown by a light wind.

"This will make a delicious stew," he said. "What a blessing to have such a thing at a time like this!"

Bob had left his section of the wall and was now kneeling beside Iwabuchi-san's brother, gently lifting the top edge of the cast and peering down into it. The brother groaned; Bob nimbly withdrew his hands, and the brother fell back asleep. He had evidently been hit by a bullet or shrapnel, because his knee was streaked with scars. One of the scars, still open just below the top of the cast, was oozing a tea-colored pus that had stained both his cast and the cloth covering his other leg below the knee.

Bob leaned across the floor, stretched his hand all the way out, and took hold of the top edge of the crate, sliding it along the ground toward him. When it was alongside him, he reached in and took out the medicine box, which was the only thing left in the crate. He opened the box and, with the tips of his fingers, picked out a small tube of cream. He put the tube's cap between his teeth and twisted it open. He squeezed some of the white cream onto his fingertip, smelled it, and gently rubbed it over the knee and down into the cast. Then he stopped, clasping his hands together below his chin, and reached back into the medicine box, taking out a little bottle of brown liquid. He twisted off the cap and smelled the liquid.

"This is iodine," he whispered to me.

"Look at his toes, Bob," I said. "The nails are all greenish, and they smell. It very well may be gangrene. His blood has stopped circulating there. I saw this when I was training as a nurse's assistant at a field hospital on Ishigaki. I think we're going to have to remove the cast."

Bob crouched forward, his eyes now nearly up against Iwabuchi-san's brother's knee. Very carefully he poured a few drops of iodine into the cap. He used the cap to pour those drops down into the cast and onto the open scar. Without warning, the brother bolted upright, bending his knee. If Bob hadn't been very quick in his reaction, the cast would have smashed right into the bridge of his nose. Luckily, he had snapped his head back immediately after pouring the iodine.

"What the . . . ! Get your damn hands off me!" hollered the brother, coughing from his fit of anger. "I told you not to touch me. Damn you! Damn you all!"

"Sorry, a-nee-kee-san, but you will die from that infection if we don't do something about it," said Bob.

The brother seemed to understand Bob's words.

"Die?" he said, alternating coughs with eerie laughs. "I can't die without taking the enemy with

131

me, don't you understand? I will not die here alone. This is a promise."

"He still seems a bit upset," said Bob to me. "Please tell a-nee-kee-san that the only thing I desire is for him to get better so that we can truly be friends, not enemies."

"Don't translate what he said," shouted Iwabuchi-san's brother in a hoarse voice. "I don't want to know what he said. I don't care what he said. When I recover, I'm going to kill him anyway."

"What did he say?" asked Bob.

"I think you're right," I said. "He's still a bit upset."

Bob smiled down at the brother, patting him on the arm.

"A-nee-kee-san," he said, "be brave and we will all get through this together. Tell him that we're all in the same boat. Do you know how to say that in Japanese? It means his fate is my fate and all our fates in one. If we die, we die together. If we live, we live together."

The brother brushed Bob's hand off with a swift jerk of his arm, leaving the gun pointed straight at Bob's face. Bob put up his hands again.

"I surrender, a-nee-kee-san. I'm yours."

The brother grumbled something that I couldn't hear clearly, pulled the gun back to his chest, turned onto his side with his back to us, wincing from the pain, and shut his eyes.

"Shikata ga nain da," ("Nothing can be done about it,") said Iwabuchi-san, stirring the rice that he had put into the stock. He added, "I'll put in the eggs last."

Bob returned to sit cross-legged in front of his wall.

"He sits for much longer than I do now," said Iwabuchi-san. "I think it gives him peace."

"Peace."

"Yes."

It was strange to hear that word. I hadn't heard it for years. People talked all the time about the war's beginning, the war's progress, and even the war's end. But no one bothered to mention peace. What, I wondered, would be the state of the world after the war, if not peace? The period of the *afterwar*, that's all it would be. War had to be in every description of an age, in every sentence spoken or thought. There was no past, present, or future; there was only before-war time, duringwar time, and afterwar time, and the three melded together like differently colored metals in an intense fire, taking a shape when the fire cooled down until the heat rose once again and a new form of the same thing was created . . . the making and remaking of time itself.

Why couldn't I predict my future, know what I would be like in the years to come, how I would act and how I would judge myself after the fact of war, when those metals that made up time had cooled and taken on a new shape? This was what was racing through my mind as I stared into the jagged-edged walls of the cave.

The only sounds in the room were those of the stew in the pot, a thick, bubbling rice gruel, and the now-irregular drip of rainwater into the pail. Both Iwabuchi-san and Bob were sitting up as straight as chopsticks in front of their own sections of wall: Iwabuchi-san's rectangular picture, Bob's round picture. The two sections somehow shone more brightly than any light in the room that they could be reflecting. It was as if those pictures had absorbed all of the light in the room from the time passed and were slowly radiating it out now. I could see the two men's faces, transparent masks, reflected in the walls' faint mirrors.

I tried to close my eyes to take a nap, but my thoughts kept awakening me each time I was on the point of dozing off. What would happen if Iwabuchi-san's brother recovered? Would he do what he had promised and kill the traitors in the cave: Iwabuchi-san, Bob, and me? Or would he leave, make his way to Ishigaki, and then bring the military police back with him?

The war could end before he got there. That was not a hope. It was only a turn of phrase. "Perhaps the war will end soon . . ." "When the war ends . . ." "After the war . . ." These words could be mouthed in the duringwar time with perfect calm. They were easy to say. No one could object to these phrases. But they expressed nothing but a nod in the direction of a hypothetical future date, time without content, the little empty box of a date on a calendar.

Bob shook me awake, though I was certain that I hadn't dozed off. I blinked several times, yawned, and turned to Iwabuchi-san's brother, who was sitting up against the wall eating with metal chopsticks from a metal bowl.

"He seems to have gotten back his appetite," said Bob to me, calling to the brother, "Bon appétit!" He turned back to me. "Maybe he understands French. Do you think?"

The brother didn't so much as acknowledge Bob's words or presence. He just continued to eat, lifting the bowl to his lips and blowing on each bite of the hot gruel.

"Hiromi-san, here's your portion," said Iwabuchi-san, handing a bowl to Bob, who, in turn, passed it to me.

"Thank you very much."

"No, it is we who have to thank you, Hiromi-san," said Iwabuchi-san. "You are now acting not only as our friend, but as our uncle." He then spoke to Bob, "Shee izu an-karu, an-karu."

"I like that. Uncle Hiromi."

Bob clasped his palms together and bowed ceremoniously. Iwabuchi-san held out another full bowl.

"Bo-bu, dozo," ("Bob, here you are,") he said.

"Thank you, Iwabuchi-san. You're a first-rate cook. Hiromi-san, please tell Iwabuchi-san that he should open up a restaurant after the war."

I translated what Bob said, and Iwabuchi-san only laughed, waving a hand at Bob as if to say, "Aw, gimme a break!"

"Yeah, I can see it now. He can call the place 'The Cave Man.' Traditional food just like you ate during the war. People will someday want to relive it. What better way than to eat the things you ate while the war was on? We can even have candlelight and dirt floors to get them in the mood."

I didn't translate this because I knew that I wouldn't be able to express Bob's ironic humor in Japanese, if it, indeed, was ironic humor. Again and again, whatever happened, whatever was said, however trivial, whatever sounds were made, even so much as a sigh, a yawn, or a groan, all things in one's life could occur solely in terms of before, during, or after the war. Was there no way to talk about oneself apart from this . . . was there no separating the metals formed in the intense fire once and for all?

Iwabuchi-san's elder brother had finished his gruel and placed his bowl beside him. Now he was fingering the gun, holding its barrel up in the little light that shone from the three candles in the room, blowing air into the trigger guard, and gently running his index finger up and down the back of the handle.

"This is a Japanese Army–issue gun. Where did the American get it, eh?"

There was silence in the room. I exchanged glances with Iwabuchi-san, realizing that a discussion about this could lead only to quarreling.

"Hear me? Did you hear what I said?" he shouted. "I asked where the American got this Japanese gun!"

"Does he want to know about the gun?" asked Bob. "He wants to know why I have a Japanese gun, doesn't he."

I nodded, afraid to look up. Iwabuchi-san slurped down the dregs of his gruel and tossed his bowl into the pot, which was now entirely empty. It broke the silence with a loud metallic clank, jolting me and making me shiver.

"Tell him that I took it off a dead Japanese soldier. The man was already dead. In fact, his head was sitting on his chest. I mean, he was like those statues you see in the museum, the ones with no heads on them. The gun still worked then. I made sure that it broke. I broke it on purpose. I didn't want to ever use it from then on. That's when I deserted. But I thought that it might be good to have for show, in case I needed it. But I would never fire a gun again. I never will. Tell him that."

I translated what Bob said.

"Even if this American didn't kill the Japanese, another American did. That makes him as much a murderer as the one who did it. He is going to pay for what other Americans did."

Having said this quite calmly, with a grin on his lips, he continued to run his finger up, down, and around the handle; over the trigger guard; and along the bottom of the barrel until he came to the muzzle. When the tip of his finger touched the muzzle, he hollered, "Bang!" and let his finger fly in Bob's direction.

"Fine, fine, you got me," is all Bob said, repeating it. "Fine, fine, you got me. I'm dead, a-nee-kee-san. You got what you wanted. I'm dead."

"I will put this cream and iodine on myself from now on. I will make myself better, without you three. Then, when I am fully recovered and can walk, I will leave here. When you see me again after that, the war will be over for you. You three should never have been here in the first place. You, you, young girl, you should be with your father, helping our brave men win this war quickly. You, you, American, you are as good as dead. But you should have died before coming here. You should, by all rights, be rotting in your grave by now. And you, you, my cowardly brother, you are the most vile of all. You, you, you have brought shame on our family name, like our weak, cowardly uncle. You make me sick in the pit of my stomach. You make me feel the deepest shame before our ancestors. You too, you too will die for His Majesty the Emperor, I promise you that. I promise you that!"

He had hollered these last words so loudly that they would surely have been heard outside. Luckily, the opening in the wall in the other room faced the grotto, where people rarely went.

The brother was now grinning openly at the three of us. I could see all of his teeth, such as they were. Four or five of the front teeth on his left side were missing. Perhaps they had been blown off by the blast that injured his leg. He was relishing the sight of us, taking us in as if he would never see us together again in that cave. I felt as if we were posing for a photograph, just for him.

Laboriously, he rose. Bob moved forward to help him, but the brother put up his palm. Bob stopped. Supporting himself on the walls, the brother hopped, without his crutch, around the curve, up to the fork in the path, and into the inner sanctum.

"I think he's really improving," said Bob. "Must be the medicine. He'll be himself in no time flat."

"I doubt it," I said. "Medicine takes a lot longer to have an effect than that."

"Yeah, maybe," said Bob. "Maybe. Yeah, who knows."

Suddenly Bob turned all pensive and glum. He kept nodding his head over and over again, and he then sat down with his back to his section of the wall, folded his arms over his chest, and shut his eyes.

Iwabuchi-san and I exchanged glances once more.

"My brother's always been like that," he said. "Think nothing of it. He's no different from a million other Japanese men. But it's you I'm worried about. Are *you* going to be all right? That's what I want to know, Hiromi-san."

"Me? Yes. Fine."

"You're only sixteen. Bob's not much older. You two are much too young to have to experience a war at such close hand."

Is this close hand? I wondered. We were not in combat. Yet, he was right. There was no escaping wartime. It didn't matter where you were. Was I sixteen? The war was taking my age from me. No matter how long I live, I thought, my age will have a single color determined by what happened here.

The sky had cleared by the time I left the cave for Mrs. Gima's house. I made my way home under a blanket of stars. I had made up my mind to gather my belongings and take them to Iwabuchi-san's uncle's house that night. It was only a little past nine o'clock, and I figured that Mrs. Gima was bound to be awake. I would have a cup of tea with her, bow to her, and tell her how indebted I was. Then I would leave that house for good.

When I arrived, candles were lit in both the living room and the room with the radio, but she was nowhere to be seen. The rake had been replaced in its crate. The sliding door to the garden had been left open, and the wind had brought in a mound of dead leaves and some thin twigs. I went into the narrow pantry at the very back of the house where there were shelves attached to the wall, just as in Iwabuchi-san's uncle's house. This pantry was much smaller in Mrs. Gima's house, though. As I turned the corner into this darkened room, I saw her immediately. Her body was hanging from a hook in the ceiling meant for the wire of a suspended lamp fixture. Her bare feet were some ten centimeters above the floor. Her body was swaying ever so slightly, perhaps from the wind coming through the door to the garden. I couldn't see her face. She had covered it with a large Okinawan scarf. Her legs were tied together with the sash of a summer kimono. The sash had the same pattern as the one I had given Bob. I took all of this in without emotion, frozen to the spot.

In a matter of seconds I found myself screaming, shrieking, calling for help, though I knew that no one was nearby to hear me. I grabbed her legs, holding them up. This unhooked the rope that was around her neck. Her body dropped straight down onto me. I was shoved against the shelves. Had I not been, I would have fallen heavily to the floor. I let her down onto the floor and uncovered her face. Her mouth was agape and her teeth were protruding out of it, like teeth on a bare skull. One of her eyes was wide open. I closed it. Her body was stiff. I could tell, without feeling the pulse on her neck, that she had been dead for some time. She must have hanged herself shortly after I left in the late afternoon. Her right hand lay in my lap. Its fist was closed. A few charred strands of her daughter's hair stuck out from between her fingers. Her hand, chin, and lips were smeared and blackened with soot. I laid her down on her back, rose, took several deep breaths, and ran out of the house on my bare feet all the way to the home of the Yoshigami sisters. They were the only people I could turn to. Their house was black inside. I slid the front door open and shouted, "Excuse me! Hello! Yoshigami-san! Yoshigami-san!" Some seconds later the elder sister appeared, then the younger sister, both in loosely tied cotton robes. They stared at me. I couldn't speak. I started to weep. My chest heaved, my voice cracked when I tried to speak. I could not tell them what I had seen. I plopped down on the floor with my head in my hands. The sisters just stood there, gazing down at me. Finally I was able to speak a few words at a time in between sobs. The sisters disappeared into their room, reemerging a minute or two later in mompe and white blouses. They lifted me up together. I was still sobbing, but in a much more subdued way than before.

When we reached Mrs. Gima's house, they went alone into the pantry, coming out immediately. They told me that it would be best to leave the body there until the morning, when it could be buried. There was no way that it could be sent for burial to another island. There were no more boats left on Hatoma Isle. No one would come here until the war ended, they said. The war had finally passed Hatoma by. We could all stay on Hatoma until the very end. We were safe. We would live. This was what they told me. I slept that night on a futon in Iwabuchi-san's uncle's living room, surrounded by books on mountain climbing in Japan and the rest of the world.

The next morning, the Yoshigami sisters and I dug a big hole in Mrs. Gima's garden and buried her in it. She had apparently been a Christian. I had never noticed the cross on the wall in a dark corner of the back room. I made a cross out of thick vines and twisted it into the ground with my bare hands. We stood in silence over the grave for a minute before the Yoshigami sisters went home. They told me to be brave, repeating what I had heard so many times yet had never ever believed: that the war would be over soon.

"Just look after yourself till it ends," they said. "Just look after yourself. That's all that matters now. The rest will take care of itself."

APRIL 8, 1945

FINE ALL DAY

After we buried Mrs. Gima, I borrowed her wheelbarrow and transported all of my bottles of star sand and the hundreds of empty bottles, together with the few personal possessions that I had, to my new home. I would return to her house to fetch vegetables from the garden and make sure that the cross was upright, but I decided that I wouldn't plant any new vegetables there. I would cultivate them in my new garden at Iwabuchi-san's uncle's house.

As I looked at the rows of bottles filled with star sand sitting on the floor against the walls of my new home, I began to wonder what purpose they had. Who would want these tiny starlike objects? What good would they do anyone? All of a sudden, the reason for continuing to collect the star sand was lost to me. But I immediately shrugged off this sense of emptiness. I would not let anything or anybody stop me from collecting it. I didn't need a reason to do something. It was important simply to keep doing what you did up till then, without going into reasons. If you were able to do today what you did yesterday without asking yourself why you continued to do it, you would somehow get through to the next day. That's what

I told myself, and, at least on that morning, I still believed it.

Iwabuchi-san's uncle's radio was in his kitchen. Perhaps he listened to it while eating. I switched it on. The imperial Japanese forces were still repelling "the cowardly attack" of the Americans, and many American soldiers were being taken prisoner. Soon they would be tried for war crimes and dealt with "under the Japanese military code of justice."

While this news was being read, I went into the pantry at the back of the house. I carried the kanpan, rice, sugar, and dried kombu seaweed into the kitchen and put it all in a small crate. I wrapped the crate in my furoshiki with ten empty milk bottles, picked up my spear, turned off the radio, and set out for the cave.

When I arrived at the beach by the grotto, I lowered the furoshiki onto the sand, placed the bottles in my string bag, and walked into the surf with my spear. I wasn't two meters into the water when I caught sight of a big ray. It was lying flat on the sand, its uniform grayish color the perfect camouflage. I saw it only because it had lifted up one of its fins, slightly disturbing the star sand on the seabed.

I raised my spear as high above my head as I could and flung it into the water. It struck the ray right in the middle of its back. The ray immediately started to swim, frantically flapping up and down, first toward me, then out to sea, my spear sticking out of the water like a fin. I dove into the water and swam as fast as I could, following the ray. My hair came undone, and my long hairpin fell onto the seabed. The ray wove around toward the grotto and then swam in a circle. It was heading out to sea. Only the tip of the handle of my spear was showing now. The water was deeper than my height. I could always make another spear, and I decided not to pursue the ray any farther. But just then the spear popped out of the water between me and the grotto. It was almost within reach. The ray swam toward the grotto but stopped short before entering it. Slowly the spear angled into the water and disappeared. I swam to it and grabbed it tightly, dragging the dead ray through the water to shore. The ray was even bigger than I had thought. This ray would provide a feast that would last the men two or three days. For that moment, I felt elated.

Leaving the ray on the hot sand with my spear sticking vertically out of it, I reentered the water, retrieved my hairpin from the seabed, curved around the grotto, and scooped up ten bottles of star sand, capping each with a piece of cloth and a rubber band. While wading back toward the shore, I stopped momentarily when the water was waist-high. The sparkling white sand of the beach in the foreground, the clumps of dense dark-green shrubbery, and the gray rock face spread out before me, with the gaping black mouth of the cave in the center. The mouth appeared all the more black for the sunlight bleaching the sand and sky. The ray wasn't moving, but for some reason, my spear tilted and fell easily, as if in slow motion, out of the wound and onto the sand.

When I presented the ray at the door of the inner cave, I had expected Iwabuchi-san to raise his hands in glee. I was also dying to tell him about the kombu. With kombu and dried bonito shavings, he could make a genuine soup stock for any kind of gruel or stew.

"Bob's malaria has come back" was the first thing he said at the door.

"Oh no," I said. "Is he all right?"

"He's not really conscious. I mean, he is conscious, but he isn't making any sense when he talks, and he obviously doesn't know where he is. I don't know what he's saying, but sometimes he just speaks for minutes on end without stopping. He says your name over and over. Anyway, come on in, quick."

He shut the door behind me and took the ray, which I had been dragging along the sand by its stinger. I put the furoshiki on a plank and knelt by Bob's side. He was fast asleep, murmuring a string of words. He fell silent. The skin on his arms and neck was covered in goose pimples. I quickly removed the crate and spread the furoshiki over his torso and legs. He mumbled something that I could not hear properly. He was rubbing the sash that I had given him, the one with the pattern of five and four on it.

Iwabuchi-san's elder brother was not in the room. I threw a glance at Iwabuchi-san and pointed to where his brother had slept. Iwabuchi-san gestured toward the back room of the cave, and I nodded. I leaned over Bob to whisper something in his ear. It was then that I noticed that he had been bleeding from the top of his head. There was a lump of blood caked into his hair and a trickle of dried blood that had run down the back of his neck.

"Did Bob hit his head again?" I asked.

Iwabuchi-san paused and then nodded once.

"Oh, the poor man."

"No, he didn't hit his head," said the brother, hobbling back into the room, supporting himself by holding on to the wall.

"Then how did he get this injury?"

"I gave it to him."

The brother grinned his sinister open-mouth grin again. I looked toward Iwabuchi-san.

"Is that true?"

"Of course it's true, why ask him?" said the elder brother. "How else do you think he got smashed on the head like that, eh? Take a look. He's got blood on his neck, too. Should've broken his skull open while I was at it."

He hobbled across to the corner of the room, wincing from the pain in his knee. He bent forward and picked up his crutch. It had been split into three sections.

"See? It's all broken. See these two sharp edges? His head broke it like this. I hit him over the head with this because he tried to touch me again with those murderer's hands. Broke my crutch in three. Now I won't be able to leave here until I can fix it. It's a real shame, because I was planning on leaving here today or sometime. This business just slows me down. But sometimes you have to do things that go against your better interests. If you really believe in something."

He snickered to himself, tossing the three pieces of his crutch to one side.

"Is this true, Iwabuchi-san?"

Iwabuchi-san nodded once, his eyes fixed on the sand.

"Why didn't you stop him?" I asked, my voice coming out in a shrill shout. "You should have stopped him!"

"I couldn't," said Iwabuchi-san, lighting a cigarette. "It all happened so fast. I was over there, sitting at my wall."

"You were staring at that stupid thing on the wall while your brother nearly killed an innocent man?"

I was surprised by my own outrage. I had never felt so angry in my entire life.

"Innocent? He's not innocent," said the brother. "He deserves what he got. And you deserve the same. I told you that. You didn't believe me. You thought I was not myself? I am myself, then, now, and until the moment I die."

I screamed. I stopped, catching my breath. I screamed again, at the top of my lungs.

"Stop it, Hiromi," said Iwabuchi-san. "You will only bring people here, and then everything will be over."

"Isn't everything over now? What else is there to do? Just eat and go to the place you call the inner sanctum and eat again and sleep and wait and wait and wait and wait? What are we waiting for? Can you answer me that? What in hell are we waiting for here?"

"For when all of this ends."

"It has ended, Iwabuchi-san, everything has ended right here. The war does not end at the same time for everyone. But it has ended here in this cave. Today. Now."

I stared at the elder brother. My hatred for him was so profound, I think I would have shot him had that gun not been broken.

I screamed. I took a breath and screamed again.

"Be quiet, Hiromi!" said Iwabuchi-san. "Please be quiet. We must not be found. Not until the war ends. It's not much longer now. You wouldn't want to do anything that you would regret later in life."

Iwabuchi-san's elder brother hopped to where I had left my spear beside the dead ray. He picked it up and, with a grotesque mask of a face, held it high in the air with both his hands, as if it were a sacred object to be worshipped.

Iwabuchi-san's words echoed loudly in my ears. "You wouldn't want to do anything that you would regret . . ."

This is where the diary ends.

PART TWO

PART TWO

REPORT ON SURVEY OF YAEYAMA ISLANDS

US MARINE CORPS

CAMP HANSEN, KIN,

OKINAWA

APPENDIX VI

HATOMA ISLE

As stated in the body of this report, the Yaeyama Islands played a relatively insignificant role in the defense strategies of the Imperial General Headquarters due to their isolation from the primary theaters of war. Consequently, this survey, the last of its kind in Okinawa, was not undertaken until 1958.

Hatoma Isle, located at N 24°28'03" E 123°49'21", has a population of between forty and fifty inhabitants, who live primarily off fishing and processing katsuobushi (blocks of dried bonito), which is used as a soup-stock flavor enhancer. Immediately after the cessation of hostilities in August 1945, the population of the island increased severalfold, declining gradually again from the time of the signing of the San Francisco Peace Treaty on September 8, 1951, until the present day.

The survey team remained for only two days on the island, judging this sufficient to establish that there had been no military presence on the island during the war. No concealed weapons were discovered, save for the odd home-fashioned bamboo spear.

There was only one discovery of a nature establishing a link with the hostilities. Facing a beach on the northern orientation of the island, a cave was found. This cave led to another cave inside it, accessed through a wooden door that was attached by hinges to the cave wall.

Inside the cave, the skeletal remains of three individuals were discovered. It was obvious to the survey team that these individuals were living or hiding out in the cave, as it was supplied with a fire for cooking, as well as a kerosene lamp, crude cooking implements, and a hole that was evidently used as a toilet in a separate area of the cave.

The description of the remains is as follows:

One skeleton dressed in a United States Army uniform.

One skeleton dressed in a Japanese Army uniform.

One skeleton dressed in a white blouse and the traditional trousers worn by farming females, known as "mompe."

All remains were collected and transported to Camp Hansen, and the remains of the two Japanese were subsequently handed over to representatives of the Japanese Administration resident in Naha. The body of the American remains at Camp Hansen.

There was nothing particularly unusual about the cave itself, save for the fact that the skeleton in the American uniform was found in a heap, as if the individual had died in a sitting position in front of what appeared to be a polished circular section of the cave wall. There was also a similar polished rectangle in the wall in front of which the skeleton in the Japanese Army uniform was located. The skeleton in female farmer attire was located in a far-back section of the cave that is closest to the ocean.

In addition to the aforementioned remains and items, the survey team also recorded the following items present in the cave:

A sharpened bamboo spear, such as those used by the Japanese Home Guard and mentioned above.

A wooden box containing candles, matches, cigarettes, and articles of men's apparel.

A broken crutch.

A small bottle of sand or pebbles.

A can of hardtack known in Japan as "kanpan," rice, powdered bean paste, sugar, dried seaweed, etc.

A diary written in Japanese. This was found on the lap of the individual in Japanese uniform.

The survey team passed the diary to the camp's Decoding Section, where it was read for possible clues that could reveal the nature of the three individuals' remains. It became clear from a reading that this diary was written by one Hiromi UMENO, a sixteen-year-old Japanese-American girl who had spent the years of her childhood in the United States. The remains of the other two individuals appear to be those of an American soldier named "Bob" and a Japanese soldier by the name of IWABUCHI. This Iwabuchi seems to have had an elder brother who visited the cave, but his remains were not located on Hatoma Isle. It is assumed that he left the island sometime in the middle of April 1945.

The above information was passed on to representatives of the Japanese Administration resident in Naha. We have received their report on the incident, as the diary of the young girl was also surrendered to them. The remains of the soldier named Iwabuchi are apparently those of Takayasu IWABUCHI, a soldier who deserted the Imperial Japanese Army at Manila in October 1944. His elder brother, Hajime IWABUCHI, was wounded in battle, but records do not indicate his whereabouts subsequent to that.

All efforts are being made to locate the identity of the American soldier named "Bob," a native of New York City. But, given that his dog tags are not extant, this is proving to be a difficult task. A record of his remains has been filed herewith at Camp Hansen until such time as the identity of this individual may be established.

Respectfully submitted,
(signed)
Major Kenneth R. Drake
Camp Hansen
Kin, Okinawa
Dated this 11th day of November, 1958.

PART THREE

PART THREE

DECEMBER 12TH, 2011

When I think that next year is going to be my last at the university, I feel a lot of anxiety. Anyway, yesterday when I ran into Professor Shiroma on campus, I had a discussion with him about my graduation thesis for next year. He has been giving me great ideas and really encouraging me to do my own original research. He's really awesome, and I'm not the only Doshisha student to think so.

Professor Shiroma was the one who got me going on my Okinawa project. I wasn't interested in Okinawa at first, but then he said a lot was still unknown about Okinawa and how the war sort of ruined life and everything for the people there. And he's been so cool, introducing me to his cousin who works for Okinawa Prefecture. I'm so excited about the e-mail I got from his cousin with a really pretty picture postcard of Okinawa attached.

To Hosaka Shiho

Greetings from Okinawa!

My name is Chinen Hitoshi and I am a cousin of your professor.

*I would be very happy to help
you with your thesis in any way I
can. We have a large storehouse
of materials, and you are free to
use them on your visit to Naha.
Welcome to Okinawa!*

In haste,

Chinen

So, I am off to Okinawa. For the very first time.
Life changes quickly sometimes!!!

It's December 24th and only seven more days till New
Year's Eve! I've already put down lots of notes for
my thesis, and I have lots of stuff still to get through.
I don't really know where it will all lead me, but it's
so exciting! I wasn't interested much in the war thing
before I took Professor Shiroma's class, and now he's
going to be my supervisor next year. That is just so
cool.

Chinen-san was SOOOO nice. He took me
around their library, which has all of these amazing
documents from the war and the Occupation period.
You could spend a lifetime, and you wouldn't even

scratch the surface of it. But he picked out something that he thought might interest me. It is the diary of a young girl, much younger than me, who wrote it when she was hiding out in a cave on a little island that I had never even heard of, Hatoma Isle, in the Yaeyama Islands of the Ryukyu chain. Her name was Umeno Hiromi. I couldn't even read the name of the island because it's so unusual, with *hato* (dove) and the *ma* that means *aida* (in between). Even Professor Shiroma has never been there!

So, I spent a day reading the diary in the library in Naha, and I was really moved by it. But, there were a few sort-of strange things about the diary that even I noticed, and I discussed them with Chinen-san, and then he referred me on to some other people, like experts, who worked in the library. That's why I ended up spending almost six whole days in Okinawa. I thought of going down to Hatoma to see the cave that Hiromi wrote about, but Chinen-san said that the American Occupation report had summed up what was left in the cave conclusively, so I decided it wasn't worth it.

But then I had discussions with those experts, and now—guess what?—they're going to open an investigation into the diary and the cave and everything. So, everything may not have been so conclusive after all.

It's really cool that my graduation thesis has started up something new.

The first thing was something I noticed. The diary was clearly written with a ballpoint pen. I thought this was really weird because I did a paper in my second year on the history of the ballpoint pen, and I knew that it was patented around 1938 by a Hungarian man named Biro and that they even call ballpoint pens "biros" in some countries. Anyway, ballpoint pens weren't used by us Japanese until after the war. I couldn't figure out how Hiromi could have written the diary with that kind of pen when she was on Hatoma in 1945.

There was another thing about it, too. The way she described things—I mean things that happened to her and things that she saw—and the way it ended all of a sudden. Her diary didn't really seem like a real diary to me.

But Chinen-san said it had to be, because it was found by the Americans in 1958 in the cave, and Hiromi's body was one of the three bodies they found there with it. So, I guess I am wrong about that. But still, the thing about the ballpoint pen is really weird.

It's already one-twenty in the morning on December 25th. I'm going to leave Kyoto tomorrow—I mean, today!—to visit my parents in Hanamaki. I'll be there for New Year's.

I got really sick with the flu when I got home and had to stay in bed for two weeks. I was miserable, but now I'm completely better and back in Kyoto. Being home was really nice, but my little brother, Tadashi, is such a pain in the neck! I couldn't find my cell when I got better, and it turns out he had it and was using it to download all sorts of stupid games. When Dad gave me the phone, he said I would have to pay for the calls and downloads, which was fine with me then. But now Tadashi is going to have to pay for all of his stupid games, except that he has no money, so Dad says he'll pay it. So, there is justice in this world!!! I really, really, really hate my brother.

When I got back to Kyoto, there was a special-delivery letter from Chinen-san waiting for me in my mailbox. I couldn't wait to read it. It was the first time ever that someone sent me a special-delivery letter!

> *I hope you are well and that you enjoyed a nice holiday with your family.*
>
> *It was truly fortuitous that you noticed the ink in the diary. Hosaka-san, you were absolutely right! Our experts, one of whom does verification of signatures and documents in*

*our courts, have determined that the
diary of Umeno Hiromi was written
in the 1950s, years after the incidents
in the cave took place.*

*This means that, if the diary was
in fact written by her, she must have
been alive after the diary ended.
But her remains were discovered in
the cave. So, it doesn't really make
sense.*

*This being the case, we have
ordered forensic tests on her remains,
or should I say, the remains of the
person thought to be her, as well as
on the remains of the soldier thought
to be Iwabuchi Takayasu. In addition,
through the Okinawa Prefectural
Office, we have contacted the
American military authorities to con-
duct a DNA test on the remains of the
American soldier who is referred to as
"Bob" in the diary.*

*This is all thanks to you, Hosaka-
san. I am writing my cousin to tell him
what a wonderful job you are doing
on your graduation thesis. When you
finish later this year, please send it to
me, and I will pass it on to another
cousin of ours who writes for the*

Ryukyu Shimpo, the newspaper here in Naha. The next time you visit us, you may be famous!

My life has turned around at least 180 degrees! And the real reason is Yutaka. He is so cool. He's been in my class all semester, but I didn't really notice him because he looks like a classic nerd. He even wears glasses that are as thick as the bottoms of two milk bottles. And he wears suspenders, too, with his jeans! How creepy is that! His family name is Kinoshita. He's two years older than me, and that's because he sort of made up his mind after his first year to drop out and learn something about life, so he went to Europe and worked in all sorts of places like restaurants and things, and he picked up—that's the phrase he used, "picked up"—French and Italian and Spanish. That is just so cool. He's not a nerd at all, he just looks like a nerd. I haven't told anyone that we both fell in love with each other, like right away, right after we had our first coffee together at Doutor by Demachiyanagi. Yutaka ordered espressos for both of us, and he did it in French! How cool is that!!!

Anyway, this morning I got an e-mail from Chinen-san in Naha. It was the most amazing one I've ever received.

*The weather in Naha is warming
up, and I assume that you will
be viewing the plum blossoms
in Kyoto about now. I was a student at Kyoto Sangyo University,
and I remember this time of year
very well. I trust that you are
healthy and enjoying your student life.*

*I hasten to report to you the vari-
ous findings that have come to
our library through the Okinawa
Prefectural Office. There are
three separate reports concern-
ing the remains found in the cave
on Hatoma Isle by the American
Marine Corps Survey Team in
1958.*

*First and foremost, it must be
said that the remains were of
three male individuals. The skeleton in the mompe and blouse
was that of a male. These were
the bones of Iwabuchi Hajime,
the elder brother of Takayasu.
The other bones belonged to
the younger brother, Takayasu.*

*It was confirmed by DNA
analysis that, virtually beyond a
shadow of any doubt, the bones
belonged to people who were
brothers.*

*The skeleton in the American
Army uniform was identified
as that of Robert Jay Rosen of
Brooklyn, New York. Thanks to
the fact that she had registered
a missing-person report with
the Department of Defense
in Washington, D.C., Robert
Jay Rosen's grandniece, Mrs.
Karen Sachs Chung of White
Plains, New York, was noti-
fied by e-mail shortly after the
identification was verified. The
remains are being flown back
to New York next week, directly
from Okinawa on a US Air Force
plane, for burial with full military
honors at a cemetery on Long
Island, New York.*

*The remains of Umeno Hiromi,
the young girl who apparently
wrote the diary, were not in the*

cave and were never located on Hatoma Isle.

What happened to her, no one knows. Maybe you should find out, Hosaka-san. Maybe you are the only person who can.

Once again, thank you very much for your wonderful research into the history of Okinawa.

Please remember me to my cousin.

Chinen Hitoshi

So many things have happened to me. The new semester started, and Professor Shiroma fell ill and had to go to the hospital. Now my supervisor has changed, and it's Professor Akimoto, who is a really unpleasant and narrow-minded-scholar type of professor, and I'm really unhappy about it. He didn't like the idea of my thesis being about Okinawa and the diary, because he said it was not scholarly enough, not like real research, just some story that happened on some island no one's heard of, and that no one even knows if the story is true or not. I told him that Professor Shiroma had already approved it, and Professor Akimoto said that he was my supervisor now and he wanted me to do something "more relevant to today." Like something economic, like the financial crisis that hit stock markets and the world, and everybody losing so much money and losing their permanent positions in companies and things like that. That's all okay for him, but I hate economics!!! Professor Akimoto says it's not economics, it's history, the real history of real people's lives. I couldn't really e-mail Professor Shiroma, because he's too sick. So, all that stuff went right down the drain. So much work for nothing . . .

That isn't all that's been happening to me. Sometimes others things do happen that change a girl's life. Yutaka and I broke up. Well, actually, I broke up with him because I found out he was going out with this other girl, an Italian exchange student. Who wants to go out with a TOTAL NERD LIKE YUTAKA! I saw him and his exchange student eating a pizza together at this Italian restaurant near Hyakumanben. That was really the last straw. I phoned him from outside the restaurant and told him I never wanted to see him again. I watched him through the window as he spoke to me, nodding. After I hung up, he told his new girlfriend something, and they both burst out laughing in a really stupid way. They're made for each other if you ask me.

But then really awesome things happen in life, too. Just days after breaking up with Yutaka, I met Umeno Hiromi!!!!!! She lives in Kyoto and has been here for many, many years.

Before today, though, at the end of Golden Week to be exact, another special-delivery letter came to me from Chinen-san. By tracing Umeno Hiromi through her father, officials at the Okinawa Prefectural Office were able to locate where she lived. This is because her father was seriously injured when the atomic bomb was dropped on Nagasaki. He became an official *hibakusha,* so he was entitled to free medical care as a radiation victim. He lived only a little more than a year, but he was visited in Nagasaki, at his hospital, by Hiromi. She gave her address to the doctors there because she was entitled to receive her father's war pension. She moved a couple of times, but each time, naturally, she registered her address in whatever Kyoto ward she lived in. Now she's living in Kamigamo, at Shobuencho, right by the Kamo River and the Botanical Garden.

I wasn't sure what would be the best way to get to know her. I didn't have a phone number or an e-mail address for her, so I wrote her a long letter telling her about myself and how I learned about her, read her diary, and found out about who was in the cave. A few days later, she wrote back and gave me her telephone number. So, I called her up, and we spoke on the phone for a short time, and she said she would meet me sometime, but not right away, because she was not feeling well. She sounded really nice on the phone!

I didn't hear from her for a few days, and then yesterday, out of the blue, she phoned me and asked if it would be convenient for me to meet her today at 5:00 p.m. at the Ota Shrine in Kamigamo. I told her I didn't know it, but she explained where it was.

I was so excited taking the subway from Imadegawa up to Kitayama. I had no idea what I should buy to give her, so I just went to a florist and got a bouquet of carnations that I really hoped she'd like.

I walked from Kitayama to the Ota Shrine, getting lost once but finally finding it. There were lots of people at the shrine, some of them old ladies. I didn't know how I would identify her, but I guessed she would be able to somehow recognize me. I was shaking, really shaking. I had never met somebody who was really out of history before.

The irises in the pond at the shrine were in full bloom, that's why there were so many people there. They are so beautiful, so purple and so many of them, too. I've never seen so many irises in one place before.

Anyway, off to one side of the pond there was an old lady in a wheelchair. Our eyes met, and she smiled. I knew it was her, not only by the smile but by the long Okinawan tortoiseshell hairpin that was sticking out of the bun in her white hair. As I walked toward her, she nodded her head over and over again, never stopping smiling at me. Tears welled up in my eyes. I felt like I really knew her so well already. I guess I did, because of the diary—the diary that was written so long ago about Hatoma Isle.

I cannot describe how wonderful and warm it felt when I stood in front of her and she took my hand and held it to her cheek. I started to sob, really sob, and I think there were tears in her eyes, too, but I couldn't see them because my own eyes were so blurry!!!

I sat down on the bench beside her wheelchair, and this is what she told me . . .

Shiho-san, is it? Yes, thank you very much for taking all this trouble to find me. I suppose that I would have told no stranger what happened so many years ago on Hatoma Isle if it hadn't been for you. Someone had to know. That's what Iwabuchi-san said.

I suppose you want to know how I was able to escape the cave. I am ashamed of what I did, and I have had deep pangs of conscience all my life, but at the time I felt that I had no choice. What do you do when you have no choice . . . when running away is not even a choice . . . when not thinking, not finding reasons for your actions is no longer possible? You cannot know what you yourself would do unless you find yourself in the same spot. What I wrote in the diary was true, except for the very last part.

When I brought the ray into the cave, Bob was already dead. He had died both of malaria and from the blow to his head dealt him by Iwabuchi-san's elder brother. It had cracked his skull. It isn't true that he was mumbling something. He was dead. He was such a gentle soul. All he wanted out of life was to live it without hurting another person. He said that if a person could do that, then that person would find true happiness in life. He accomplished that at a time when it was nearly an impossible thing to do.

Iwabuchi-san didn't know what to do after Bob died. He couldn't turn his brother in to the military police, and he didn't have it in him to kill his brother either, even though he was stronger than his brother at the time and could have easily done it. Like Bob, he was a man who had come to the point where he would rather be killed than kill. What does it take to become a person like that? How long does it take to get to that point, Shiho-san? I don't know, and I will never know.

When I arrived back at the cave with the dead ray that day, the two brothers were arguing in a very violent manner. They apparently had been arguing for a couple of hours, saying the same things over and over again. Iwabuchi-san was calling his brother a cold-blooded murderer. The brother was calling him a traitor and a disgrace to Japan. He said it was a hero's deed to kill an American. Only a traitor would protect an enemy.

For each man, what the other was committing was the worst crime imaginable. There was no way of reconciling this at that time and in that place. The cave walls were no protection against the war. The air in that small, confined space had become the same air that permeated all Japan. Being brothers changed nothing. In fact, it only made the situation worse for both men. In the end, you come to hate your own more than you hate others. And it was the end, at least there and then.

Not long after I arrived, the argument seemed to simmer out. But I could see that the elder brother was still enraged and that his rage was growing more and more intense for being held in check. Iwabuchi-san's way of calming down was to blot out the cares of this world, to sit in the lotus position in front of his wall and stare at it. That was exactly what he was doing when his brother suddenly picked up a piece of his crutch, one that had a sharp end to it, and thrust it deep into Iwabuchi-san's bare back.

Iwabuchi-san turned his head once toward his brother without crying out or saying a word, though the pain must have been unbearable. The brother removed the crutch from Iwabuchi-san's back and, baring his teeth, thrust it in once again with even greater force, shouting at the top of his lungs, "Long live His Majesty the Emperor!" This time Iwabuchi-san didn't even turn toward him. He just stared at his shining black wall with his eyes wide open.

I could see that the brother was going to continue to stab and slice into Iwabuchi-san's flesh until he killed him, so, while the brother had his back to me, I lifted up my spear. Iwabuchi-san, who could see me out of the corner of his eye, shook his head and cried, *"Yamero!"* ("Don't do it!") I suppose that he did not want me to live with the memory of having killed a person. But I heaved the spear anyway, with all my might.

My spear struck the brother under his right arm and sank into his body. He turned toward me with a face of fury I have seen only on the Nio-sama statues that guard the gates at temples in Kyoto. A torrent of blood gushed out of the wound, spraying the sand and flowing down his right side. He fell against the wall and collapsed in a heap on the ground. The spear must have pierced a lung, because he was soon choking for breath. He vomited blood for a few minutes, inhaled once, and died. His blood formed a half circle in the sand around him. Iwabuchi-san and I buried his brother and Bob in the sand beside each other, shoulder to shoulder.

Iwabuchi-san was badly wounded. I nursed him with his uncle's medicines as best I could. We lived together in the cave for a week. The only times I went out were to catch fish for us. But he contracted blood poisoning, and his health began to deteriorate sharply. I wanted to do something for him, anything. I wanted to go to the Yoshigami sisters and beg for aid. But he said that there would be nothing they could do. There were no medicines on the island for blood poisoning, which he had seen other men get in China, Burma, and the Philippines, where he had fought. Besides, the Yoshigami sisters might eventually turn me in to the military police after he died. So we stayed together in the cave until he passed away, a week after Bob and his brother. I buried him in the sand beside them.

"Is that when you wrote the diary?" I asked, before recalling that it couldn't have been then because of the ink.

No.

"What did you do after Iwabuchi-san died?"

I contemplated suicide. I could have killed myself there and then. I was sure that no one would ever find us. Our story would never be known to anyone. That was one way, I thought, to take the war out of our lives forever and ever. What good would it do to tell people about what happened in that little cave on the little island far away from everywhere? What could it ever mean to people?

But I didn't. I didn't kill myself. People say of themselves in wartime, "I didn't have the courage to kill myself." Is it courageous or cowardly to kill oneself? I don't know. But I do know that, even then, long before I wrote the diary, I wanted someone to learn of the bravery of Iwabuchi-san and Bob. They *were* brave. I am not, however. I am just someone who had the privilege of spending a short time in her life with two people who were.

So, I dug up the remains of Iwabuchi-san's brother and removed the cast from his leg. Then I put my mompe and blouse on him before reburying him. I put on some clothes that were in the box, left a bottle of star sand on top of Iwabuchi-san's sand grave as a symbol of myself and my life on Hatoma in the cave, and simply walked away, shutting the driftwood door tightly behind me and stacking some big rocks in front of it so that no one would ever come across it. I stood on the shore and threw the cast into the water, watching it as it drifted out to sea. Then I went back to Mrs. Gima's house to live, where I remained until the war ended.

After my father died in Nagasaki, I chose to live in Kyoto because this city wasn't bombed during the war and I thought I could delete every trace of the war that was left in me by coming here. I made contact with my mother, who was still alive. My grandparents had died while living in the camp, and my brother had become a pilot. He was shot down somewhere over France and was never found. He is still listed as "missing in action."

My mother came to live with me in Kyoto. She taught English to little children. She didn't really like living in Japan, but I guess she chose to stay with me. She died in 1976. I took her ashes back to Los Angeles, where she wanted to be buried next to her parents, and I even stayed there for a few months, thinking I might live permanently in America. But something was drawing me back to Japan, and I returned to Kyoto. I had no family in America anymore, no one who could imagine what

I had been through. I wanted to live with people like me.

"But how did the diary get there? I mean, when did you write it?"

I wrote the diary, exactly as I remembered everything, here in Kyoto, starting in 1951 and finishing the next year. It's all true, except for the ending. But it wasn't until 1956 that I was able to make a trip back to Hatoma.

"So you went back to Hatoma?!"

Yes. And back to the cave, too. But just getting to the island involved a rigmarole! You had to get permission from the Americans, and it took weeks. But seeing as I was half-American myself and had an American passport, they really couldn't stop me. I just told people that I wanted to go back to Ishigaki to gather my aunt's things.

I got a ride on a fishing boat at Ishigaki, and the fisherman took me to Hatoma. I paid him in dollars. People were still catching a lot of fish around Hatoma at that time: tuna, bonito, rays, and fish like that. And the dried bonito factory had started up again after the war. I don't know how many people were living on Hatoma then, but it seemed like many more compared to when I had been there. Most of them were new people. They had gone down there to get away from the postwar destitution in other parts of Japan. On Hatoma, at least it was warm and you could eat.

The only person I met who I knew from before, even though only eleven years had gone by, was the younger Yoshigami sister. She was still alive. When I visited her, though, she seemed to not want to talk to me. She was very frail. She greeted me and apologized for not inviting me into her house. She asked me just one question, however.

"What was that?"

Where I was going all that time on the island. I was sure she had known I was going to the cave.

"What did you answer her?"

I told her . . . nowhere. I was going nowhere. She nodded, as if she understood. To this day I don't know whether she knew about the existence of the cave or not.

That night, I went back to the cave. Despite the number of people on the island, no one went to the beach on the northern end of it at night. It was very strange, climbing over the rocky point and standing on that beach. Nothing had changed. The grotto was still there, the sand that was white even at night, the dense shrubs, the dark-gray rock face, the round black mouth of the cave, and the Milky Way flowing like a river made of millions of tiny grains of sand stretching from one end of the sky to the other.

I entered the mouth of the cave. The rocks that I had placed in front of the door had not been moved. I opened the door. The hinges creaked now. Iwabuchi-san had oiled them when he was living there. I had the diary with me. I unearthed Iwabuchi-san's remains and carefully sat the skeleton in front of his black mirror, putting the diary and the bottle of star sand in his lap. Then I dug up Bob's remains and managed to sit his skeleton up in front of his black mirror. I left Iwabuchi-san's brother's remains where I had buried them, and, without even taking the time to look around, walked out of the cave. I felt no nostalgia, no sadness, no emotion at all when I closed the door behind me.

She stopped speaking for a moment and gazed out over the tops of the irises. There were only a handful of people by the pond now. A chilly wind had begun to blow. I looked down at her lap. There was a small bottle on it.

"Oh, I almost forgot," I said. "These are for you."

I handed her the bouquet of carnations that I had put down on the bench next to me.

"How very kind of you, Shiho-san! They are lovely."

She put them on her lap, still holding on to the bottle.

"And this is for you. It's a bottle of star sand that I collected on Hatoma during the war."

She took my hand and closed my fingers around the bottle. It had a little checked cloth top, fastened by a rubber band.

"This is the only bottle of star sand that I took away from Hatoma. I want you to have it, Shiho-san. It's for you. It's the only one left."

"Thank you very much. But what shall I do with it?"

Just when she was about to answer me, a man who looked to be in his midsixties approached us from the side.

"Mother," he said, "it's time to go."

"Shiho-san, this is my son, Takayasu. I gave him the same name as his father."

"How do you do?"

"Thank you for being so kind to my mother," he said, smiling and stroking his mother's white hair.

"You know, Shiho-san, it's a kind of miracle that we two met, don't you think?"

"I don't know. But I do think it's a miracle, too."

Her son grasped the handles of the wheelchair, swiveled it around, and, slightly lifting it over the stepping-stones that stuck out of the ground, pushed it through the little wooden gate at the entrance to the pond.

It was quite dark by then, and I wanted to get home as quickly as possible. I had not brought a jacket or sweater for myself and was shivering from the chill in the air. I turned around once, but I could not see Umeno-san anywhere.

I ran to the subway station at Kitayama as fast as I could, clutching the bottle of star sand to my chest.

ABOUT THE AUTHOR

 Roger Pulvers is an author, playwright, theater director, and translator. He has published more than forty-five books in English and Japanese, including novels, essays, plays, and poetry. He also translates works from Japanese, Russian, and Polish.

Productions of Pulvers's plays have run in the United States, Japan, and Australia, including his translation and adaptation of Nikolai Gogol's *The Government Inspector* at the Sydney Opera House. He regularly appears on television and radio in Japan, and he wrote and hosted the popular weekly NHK television show *Gift E-Meigen*.

Pulvers is the recipient of several literary prizes, including the Kenji Miyazawa Prize (2008) and the Noma Award for the Translation of Japanese Literature (2013).

He originally wrote *Star Sand* in Japanese and first published it in that language in 2015.